IN CASTLE ROBOTNIK

More ultra-cool Sonic stories!

Already published:

SONIC THE HEDGEHOG IN ROBOTNIK'S LABORATORY
SONIC THE HEDGEHOG IN THE FOURTH DIMENSION
SONIC THE HEDGEHOG AND THE SILICON WARRIORS

SONIC THE HEDGEHOG
IN CASTLE ROBOTNIK

Martin Adams

Virgin

First published in 1994 by
Virgin Books
an imprint of Virgin Publishing Ltd
332 Ladbroke Grove
London W10 5AH

Cover design by The Design Clinic

Cover illustration by Neil Rowe

This one's for Jack Johnson.
Knock 'em dead, kid.

Typeset by Phoenix Photosetting, Chatham, Kent
Printed and bound by
Cox & Wyman Ltd, Reading, Berks

ISBN 0 426 20405 0

CONTENTS

THE SONIC STORY SO FAR

There was a time when Mobius was a peaceful world. And the Green Hill Zone was the most peaceful and pleasant and generally all-round cool place to hang out on the entire planet.

Mobius's inhabitants were, and are, talking animals of all types. The hippest, streetwisest dude of all was, and is, a hedgehog named Sonic.

And of course it just had to be Sonic who stumbled into the laboratory of Mobius's only human, the kindly but absent-minded Doctor Kintobor.

Dr K was perfecting a device – the Retro-Orbital Chaos Compressor – to attract all the evil on Mobius and contain it within six emeralds he called the Chaos Emeralds (neat name, Doc). He found the time to help boost Sonic's already radically fast footwork, too, and with the help of a special pair of drop-dead cool red trainers, Sonic exceeded the speed of sound. And he turned blue, of course.

Sonic superspeeded all over Mobius, searching for the Grey Emerald that would neutralise the evil contained

in the Chaos Emeralds. But before he found it, Doctor Kintobor's absent-mindedness brought disaster to the whole planet as he entered faulty data into the ROCC. The device exploded, releasing the Emeralds, scattering protective golden rings across the length and breadth of Mobius, and transmogrifying Kintobor into his exact opposite: the evil, power-crazed, obese and egg-loving Doctor Robotnik.

Robotnik's influence reached across the entire planet. Once-verdant landscapes were transformed into polluted wastelands. The evil Doctor's robots scoured the land for animals to imprison, and in particular for the one super-fast hedgehog who has the power to foil his plans – Sonic.

And Sonic has foiled Robotnik's plans – at least twice, by the time you read this book. But Robotnik is ineggshaustibly, eggsasperatingly resilient. Once again, he's back. And that means trouble for Mobius in general, and for hedgehogs with red trainers in particular.

1

TERROR IN THE DARK

It was a dark and stormy night.

Thunder crashed from the broiling black clouds that blotted out the moon. Jagged forks of lightning lit up the night sky in garish electric blue. Raindrops the size of lightbulbs splattered into the soggy ground. Forlorn trees swayed in the howling winds, and unfortunate owls, desperately clinging on to them with cramped feet, went 'Wooooo, wooooo, wooooo!' rather pathetically. Let's face it, only a complete maniac would be outdoors on a night like this.

Sonic the world-famous hedgehog and his chums cowered in the darkness, their eyes as wide as dinner plates. Their bodies were lit only by the sinister blue flicker from the screen they were watching. Just in time, Sonic stopped Sally Acorn from squealing by stuffing a pawful of tortilla chips into her mouth.

'Begone, hideous nightmare-type being from our over-paid and totally useless special-effects department, untroubled by intelligence or creativity!' snarled the actor

on the screen. Well, no all right, that's what he wanted to say, but what he actually said was, 'Begone, foul fiend of the night! Drink the blood of the living no more!'

'Oh, gross,' Sally whimpered, gulping down the last of her unexpected snack. 'This is really scary.' Her bushy squirrel's tail stood bolt upright, as if some practical joker had just zapped forty thousand volts through it.

'Yikes!' squeaked the fox next to her. This was Miles Prower, also known as Tails, also known as Sonic's twin-tailed foxy best friend, fellow adventurer and all-round cute little dude. 'Look at that! He's got fangs bigger than Joe's!'

'We walruses do not have fangs,' Joe Sushi sniffed in mock grumpiness. 'We just have very, very large, long, sharp, pointy tusks. All the better to – eat you all up!' With that he lunged at Tails, who took super-fast evasive action sideways. Joe carried right on by him and flippered a slice of tuna and anchovy pizza into his mouth, which was what he'd really been after all the time.

'Now look, you guys! Can we all chill out and have some quiet here?' Sonic complained, tapping a red-sneakered foot irritably on the floor. 'I mean, I'm enjoying this.'

'Uuurggh! Look at all that blood!' groaned Johnny Light-foot, shielding his eyes from the video. Sonic looked over at him, a despairing look on his handsome hedgehoggy face. For a rabbit who thought he was really cool, Johnny's rating on the wimpometer was bouncing suspiciously in the red.

'He's a vampire,' Sonic pointed out. 'What do you expect him to do? Go to the mall and get a sandwich from the deli? He's just eating on the hoof, that's all. Rolling buffet, you know.'

The screen went black for a few moments, then a hideous wailing scream filled the room. All the animals – yes, even Sonic! – almost jumped right out of their skins.

'I don't want to watch this any more. This is too scary,'

Sally complained. 'I'm going to have bad dreams after watching this! It's even more scary than the one we saw last week. What was it called? *The Scrunchback of Dotty Name*?'

'Oh yeah, that was righteously cool! I loved the bit where the girl Desmerelda is ironing Quasirobo's shirt with a wok,' Sonic grinned.

Tails's eyes were glued to the screen. He wagged his twin tails ever so slightly, fascinated and scared at the same time. The video was very dark and it wasn't clear what was happening. He had to get up really close to take a good look. The cloaked vampire suddenly burst into focus on the film as lightning flared out behind him and Tails leapt two metres backward, landing flat on his back. He had his paws firmly clasped over his eyes.

Sonic stood over him, shaking his head. 'Garlic pizza?' he suggested.

'Well, I think I'm off home to bed,' Porker Lewis said with an exaggerated yawn, rubbing his eyes with his trotters. 'Although I'll probably get soaked in the rain. Gosh, it's raining cats and dogs out there.'

'Why do people say that?' Sonic wondered aloud.

'I haven't got a clue. They could have said it's raining hedgehogs and foxes, I suppose. Don't ask me.'

'Be sure the vampires don't get you,' piped up Chirps Chicken.

'Huh! There aren't any real vampires,' the pig sniffed derisively. 'Everyone knows that. I read a book about it once.'

The friends all turned to Porker, curiosity lighting up their eyes. Porker read a lot of books and he was smart, so he Knew About Stuff.

'One reason why people used to believe in them was because once, a long, long time ago, people used to be buried before they were really dead. By mistake. 'Cause

6

they got some sort of nasty lurgy that made them all look dead. Then they used to try to claw their way out of their coffins,' the pig said with relish. The others were getting more scared by Porker than they were by the film.

'So they had blood all over their hands and faces, and when they were . . . dug up,' Porker said, pronouncing those last two words v-e-r-y s-l-o-w-l-y to gross them out, 'people thought they were vampires.'

'Oh yuck! Horrible! I don't think we wanted to know that, Porker!' Sally complained.

'It's all right, I'm just going,' gloated the pig. 'Tomorrow I'll tell you what was in the second chapter of the book. Heh, heh, heh.' He flung open the door of Sally Acorn's cottage just as another flash of lightning crackled over-head. Unfurling his umbrella, he vanished into the darkness of the Green Hill Zone, closing the door behind him.

The video ended soon afterwards. They were all a little twitchy and scared, after what Porker had told them, and the storm was still raging outside. Sally asked them if they'd like to stay for the night since the weather was so bad, and everyone thought that was a good idea. Sonic thought it was an especially good idea because he'd seen Sally bringing home a twelve-pack of potato chips and a huge pack of marshmallows that afternoon and he knew where she always hid them. Sonic and slumber parties seemed to go hand in hand.

Joe, though, decided to go home. 'I don't mind wet weather,' he pointed out. 'I am a walrus, after all. I love it!' He lumbered out into the night, ducking his whiskered head through the doorway, splashing happily along through the huge pools of rainwater.

The animals settled down to sleep, dozing in Sally's comfortable armchairs. It wasn't easy to drop off, because the storm was noisier than a grunge band practising next door and they were all still a bit queasy about vampires.

Then there came a rap at the door. Bang. Bang! Bang! BANG!

Instantly Sonic jerked into wakefulness and looked at Tails. The fox put his paws over his eyes and sat hoping that whatever was at the door would go away. Sonic wasn't afraid, though, and he walked right up and flung open the door.

Wind and rain howled into his face in a sudden storm squall. He could barely see the huge, sinister form filling the doorway, its terrible twin fangs gleaming in the light of the full moon suddenly revealed by a parting in the clouds. The lumbering thing towered over him and reached down as if to grab him in its amorphous limbs.

'Better come quick, Sonic. It's Porker,' Joe Sushi said grimly. 'He's been bitten by a vampire.'

2

A VISITOR IN THE NIGHT

It was another dark and stormy night.

In fact, it was even darker and stormier than the first dark and stormy night. The thunder was so loud that a small group of field mice caught out in it had to get hearing aids to go with their white sticks after being right underneath one massive thunderclap. The sky was electric blue pretty much all the time, the lightning was so bad. Raindrops the size of watermelons splattered into the ground. Those owls were getting cramp in their legs from clinging on to the trees for dear life, and the trees dug in with their roots and hoped like crazy that the storm would soon be over. Let's face it, only a complete and utter barmpot of a maniac would be outdoors on a night like this. Oh look: here he comes now!

The cloaked figure prowled the margin of the Green Hill Zone, sticking to the undergrowth to hide his bulk. He had stalked his target carefully. He knew when to strike. The evil face cracked into a smile of evil pleasure as he contemplated his raid. It would all be over so soon, so very soon.

The dark cloak of the horror flapped about him in the howling gale. Great scurries of leaves whipped up around him as the night stalker crunched through the undergrowth on his heinous mission. At last he reached his destination. In his dark-gloved hands, he gripped the door handle, and threw open the door behind which his unsuspecting victim lay.

The squirrels inside screamed and cowered back on their settee. The remote control for the video fell from one set of paws and a bucket of popcorn fell from the other. The female squirrel screamed again, and then fainted. The other squirrel shrank back even further, trying to disguise himself as part of the pattern on the settee cover. It was a pretty good plan in the circumstances, but it didn't work.

The gloating horror advanced into the room. It was dark, sinister, utterly evil. It was also wet, with a really gross drop hanging on the end of its nose, and there were little dribbles of egg white on its waistcoat. The horror wasn't just fat. It was spherical.

'Kevin, you're coming with me. Ha ha ha!' it said.

Sonic and Joe carried the prostrate pig back to Sally Acorn's house. They laid him out on the floor, with a fluffy cushion under his head, trying their best to make him comfortable.

'Look, Sonic,' Joe growled. 'Look at the side of his neck!'

Sonic whistled through his teeth. 'I can't believe this, it's just too heinous,' he snapped. 'Vampires? In Green Hill Zone?' He bent down to take a closer look. The twin puncture marks on the side of the pig's neck were very clear.

Tails rushed in from Sally's kitchen with a hammer and a long, thick length of wood which had been hastily whittled to a sharp point at one end.

'It's terrible, Sonic, but we might have to do it!' he bab-

bled. 'It's the only way to kill vampires, you know. We saw it on the film.'

'Whoa! Chill out, little buddy,' warned the hedgehog. 'He's breathing. Just go and get me a bucket of ice.' Tails reluctantly put his weapons down and sped off.

When he returned with the few ice cubes Sally had left in her fridge, he gave them to Sonic, and stood back with a slice of garlic pizza defiantly held out in his paws. Sally thought she heard a foxy whisper of 'Begone, foul fiend!' but she wasn't certain.

Sonic stuck the ice cubes down Porker's shirt. The pig twitched and groaned.

'Oh no! He's undead! The horror! The horror!' shrieked Tails.

'Cool it!' Sonic yelled. 'Look!' Porker's eyes opened and then he scrabbled to his feet, arms flailing as he tried to get the ice cubes out of his clothes.

'What kind of practical joke is this?' yelled a furious pig.

'Keep back,' Tails warned, waving his garlic pizza. 'We have a stake and mallet and we aren't afraid to use them!'

'Has he gone mad?' Porker wondered, trying to make sense of the mayhem around him. 'I wake up here and find myself being threatened by an insane fox armed with a pizza. What kind of a welcome is that?'

Sonic looked closely at the disorientated pig. 'What do you remember, Porker?'

'Like, when?'

'Like, just this evening,' the hedgehog replied, tapping his foot irritably.

'Well, we were just watching the video, and we fell asleep, and I suppose Foxface over there must have had a bad dream and it's turned his head,' Porker replied. 'Mind you, some of us have always thought he was a bit, well, unstable,' he added darkly.

11

Tails bristled, but Sonic wasn't taking any notice. 'You don't remember walking home, do you?'

'I told you, I fell asleep. If I'd gone home, I'd have got very wet.' The pig looked down at the puddle of water he was lying in. 'Ugh, I do appear to be very wet. You dastardly hedgehog! How much ice did you use?'

Sonic helped the complaining pig up on to his trotters and manoeuvred him gently to the bathroom. He picked up Sally's vanity mirror and showed Porker the marks on his neck. The pig's terrified eyes met his own.

'I hate to say this, Porker, my old chum and all that, but would you mind trying a piece of that garlic pizza Tails has over there?'

'Well, that's a relief,' Sally Acorn sighed when they'd put Porker into the bed in her spare room. 'He can eat garlic, anyway. So he can't be a vampire.'

'Don't you believe it,' Tails whined. 'It doesn't happen instantly, you know. First he'll get all pale and weedy, and then –'

'He's fairly pale and weedy anyway,' Johnny Lightfoot pointed out.

'Well, he'll get more pale and weedy. And thin,' Tails said triumphantly, since no one could possibly fail to notice if Porker got thin. 'Then he'll get allergic to garlic, and we won't see any reflection of him in the mirror, he'll start prrrrrowling at night, and then – oh crikey! What are we going to do?'

They all looked at Sonic. At times like this, he had to take the lead.

'We'll have to find out what happened to him,' Sonic said seriously. 'Find out what kind of heinous dweeb bit him. Maybe it was one of the monkeys sneaking up from the Emerald Hill Zone playing a practical joke. Yeah, that's the likeliest thing, dudes.'

It was almost dawn outside. The storm had played itself out, and it was clear and fresh all over the Green Hill Zone.

'Hey! It's a lovely morning,' Tails said. 'Why don't we go and find those monkeys now?'

'Because I'll get my sneakers wet and muddy and that's too heinous a possibility to consider,' Sonic sniffed.

'You must go!' Sally cried. 'If something awful really has happened to Porker, it's up to you to act now and save his bacon!'

Sonic raised an eyebrow.

'Well, okay, perhaps that wasn't the most tactful way to put it,' Sally said hastily. 'But if Tails is right, we have to know now. We can't wait!'

'She's right, my most triffic hero buddy,' Tails insisted, putting on his most pleadingest face.

Sonic took the hint. Taking in a deep breath and really puffing out his chest, he took a sneak peek in the mirror to make sure his spines were really neat, and dashed out the door. Tails was right behind him.

They were halfway to the Emerald Hill Zone when they saw the last of the vampire bats fleeing to its dank and dismal home before the sun rose. Obviously, they didn't actually know it was a vampire bat from such a distance, but by now they regarded bats of any kind as seriously suspicious, given what had happened to Porker.

'Never seen any of them around here,' Tails said anxiously.

'Too right. I don't think it's, like, one of those fruit bats that eat the bananas in the Emerald Hill Zone. It's not flying that way either. Let's take a closer look,' Sonic replied. As the fox's twin tails began spinning, raising him into the air, Sonic took a run up and hit SuperSpin.

They got close enough to see that what they'd thought was a bat didn't really look right. It moved rather stiffly and its joints didn't seem natural. The main giveaway, though, was that there was a small jet engine mounted underneath its wings. When it saw them, the Batbot spun round and opened its jaws. Two long fangs presented themselves to the advancing dudes.

'Yikes!' Tails cried out, taking evasive action. Halfway through his spin, Sonic decided just to tackle the problem head-on. Gritting his teeth to get above the Batbot as it turned and swooped, he stomped it hard on the back. It fell apart into several chunks of metal which disappeared into the trees below.

'Crikey! What was that?' Tails wondered when they'd returned to the safety of the ground.

'It's got to be something Robotnik's dreamed up,' Sonic grimaced. 'I mean, who else builds heinously fiendish robots to give us a bogus time?'

'But why this? What's fatty doing now?' Tails puzzled.

'Well, my furry foxy buddy, who's going to find out? Let's get searching for those robot parts,' Sonic said, looking at the forest around them.

'Oh, Sonic, that's not going to be much fun. They could be anywhere in there. It'll take ages. And it's nearly breakfast time,' Tails pointed out.

'Hmmm,' Sonic mused. 'You're right. We'd have to spend an awful lot of time, and we'd get hungry, wet, and miserable. So here's what we'll do instead: I'll go and talk to Mickey the Monkey and find out if he knows anything about this, and you go and search for those robot parts. That way, we don't both get to be hungry and wet and miserable.'

'But why do I have to do it?' Tails whimpered.

'Because my sneakers are already getting a little damp around the edges, dude, and that is totally uncool. See you back at Sally's. Cowabunga!'

A racing hedgehog vanished in the direction of Emerald Hill Zone. Tails sniffled a bit and then slunk off into the woods. Then he had a Clever Idea.

3

ROBOTNIK EGGSPLAINS

Dr Ivo Robotnik, maniacal and demented (but occasionally brilliant) scientist and all-purpose would-be ruler of the planet Mobius, sat back and admired his most recent piece of work. The robot was an odd shape. It certainly didn't look much like the squirrel inside it, and it had a hunched back, but the Mark II Eggor was fully programmed and this time the mad genius was sure that the Total Obedience Circuits were going to work perfectly.

Robotnik had thought long and hard about Eggor. At first he wanted to send squads of Buzzers and other robots to despatch Kevin, the bright-eyed squirrel he'd once imprisoned inside the Mark 1 version and forced to help him with his experiments – just as Sonic the hedgehog helped him, once upon a time. He knew something had to be done about Kevin. The squirrel-turned-robot might Know Too Much about his, well, eggsperiments, having helped him so often. It was the same reason Robotnik was so scared of Sonic, and desperately wanted to destroy him. But simply disposing of the squirrel would have been a

15

waste of all that he'd taught him, so he had decided to
kidnap him and imprison him in robot form again. This time,
though, it was going to work. It would be perfect. It was
going to be truly eggsceptional.

'Eggor, come here!' the white-coated scientist ordered,
dribbling the last of his favourite raw-egg supper over his
fingers. The robot dutifully clanked across the floor of
Robotnik's huge laboratory.

'Now sit down at that computer – here, that's right.
Eggor, can you remember how to program the co-
ordinates for FAROUT?' Robotnik wanted to see if the
robot could remember anything of its work on the original
Fabulously Advanced Robotnik's Original Universal
Transmogrifier. Robotnik had abandoned that line of
research after Sonic had destroyed his beautiful, wonderful, lovely lovely Transmogriplex, his machine for turning
all the animals of Mobius into robots, but now he had
another fiendish plan. None the less, this was a useful way
to test out the new version of Eggor.

Eggor's metal hands tapped in a stream of keyboard
strokes into the computer, and numbers and strings of
weird characters flashed up on the screens before
Robotnik's delighted eyes.

'Eggscellent! Eggsquisite! You do remember, don't
you?' Robotnik cheered, and he wobbled up and down in
delight.

'I do your bidding, master,' replied Eggor in the new,
really deep voice Robotnik had given him.

'So you do, good robot. Ha ha ha! Well, Eggor, I have a
Brilliant Plan! I have finally found the perfect way of
eggspunging that hateful wretch, Sonic the hedgehog!
And, at the same time, ha ha ha! I shall achieve a still
further objective – winning, at last, the Mobius Prize for
Film Production and Direction!'

'But, Master, you award all the Mobius Prizes. You could

award it to yourself at any time you wished to,' Eggor said with the very slightest hint of uncertainty in his voice. Robotnik should have taken warning from that, but he didn't. He was too deeply absorbed in his fantasy.

'No, no, you silly robot! I cannot give myself the prize until I have actually made a movie! Now, look,' he said, and his porky fingers jabbed at the keyboard before Eggor, 'this is the design for the film set, and construction is almost complete! Already, some of my film eggstras have been travelling through Mobius looking for, um, the right actors.' The madman laughed maniacally. 'You, too, will have a good part in the movie, Eggor!'

'Thank you, master,' Eggor said in his flat voice.

'Of course, I shall play the leading role. *Castle Robotnik*, the movie is going to be called. A film crew is already preparing some of the opening scenes. There were a few teething troubles with some, er, pilot eggsperiments but they have all been sorted out now.' Robotnik did not need to tell his robot assistant that sorting out problems meant melting down robots that had failed him.

'It is a horror film, Eggor!'

'Good, master.' Eggor Mark II was still trying to figure out exactly what was happening. Stray thoughts about a hoard of nuts and a brood of bushy-tailed children kept drifting through his programming.

'And not only am I going to make the best movie ever made, not only am I going to get rid of that pesky hedgehog forever, but at the same time I am going to conduct a truly staggering scientific experiment for which I shall award myself the Mobius Prize for Advanced Scientific Genius – '

'For the fifth time!' Eggor eggsclaimed.

– for the sixth time. I won it again while you were, er, on holiday, Eggor. While you were being converted into a Mark II Eggor. Anyway, I shall be doing all these things at the same time! Ah, such genius, Eggor!'

'Yes, master.'

'Now, Eggor, you must learn your lines. That is very important. Movies have scripts, Eggor, and there is to be no making things up as you go along. We must use the principles of Method Acting,' Robotnik said very pompously.

'Method Acting, master?'

'Yes. Follow my method or you get melted down for scrap.'

'I have just plugged myself into the script memory bank, master,' said Eggor hurriedly. 'Ahy, yes, what syntactically precise dialogue! What mastery of words!' Eggor's Scientist-Flattering Circuit was plainly working.

'Of course, Eggor. That's because I wrote it. This will win me the Mobius Prize for Literary Composition too.'

'For the eighth time!'. Eggor congratulated him. Robotnik stiffened. Given his egg-shaped body, one might have wondered whether stiffening would have turned him into a meringue, but it didn't.

'For the ninth time, actually,' the scientist said angrily. 'Make sure you update the Robotnik Achievement Register into your databanks, Eggor. You must be able to congratulate me accurately in future.'

Eggor's Scientist-Flattering Circuit was already at work updating itself.

Sonic was deep in conversation with his friend Mickey the Monkey. Mickey was an odd sort of a dude – he didn't call him 'friend', but usually odd things like 'me old china' – but Sonic did his best to understand him and, by and large, provided the hedgehog brought along lots of peanuts and crisps, they got along well. This was because Mickey was a real wizard with anything mechanical.

'Funny you should mention it, squire, but we have seen a few funny-looking dogs and cats flying in the trees these last few days,' Mickey pondered.

'Dogs and cats? Flying? I know it was raining, but I thought it was just a figure of speech.' Sonic was understandably confused.

'Rhyming slang, me old cuppa. Dogs and cats, bats. It's like we say: slugs and snails, Sonic and Tails.'

'Oh yeah, I get it.' Sonic got it, not at all pleased to be thought of as a slug.

'Funny looking things, these bats' Mickey said. 'They don't stop and eat fruit either. They can fly awfully fast at times. Some of them', he continued, 'have been seen flying off to the Scrap Brain Zone.'

'I don't like the sound of that,' Sonic fretted.

'No. Well, since you destroyed Robotnik's laboratory down there, it's been very dangerous. Chock-a-block with mindless robots crawling all over the place. Even one or two of those Clucker things, the really nasty ones. We don't go there anymore.'

'If that's where those Batbots are going, someone's going to have to check it out,' Sonic thought aloud. 'Unless . . .'

He suddenly had a Clever Idea, and set off at an alarming speed to try it out. Racing around on the beach beside the azure waters, he shot up a palm tree, leaving a hail of coconuts spraying through the air behind him. One of them narrowly missed hitting Mickey full on the head. The monkey sat with his paws clasped over his head to protect himself. He shut his eyes tight.

When he opened them, Sonic was zipping past him leaving the words 'Wrong tree!' hanging on the air as he disappeared into the distance.

Very soon afterwards, our heroic hedgehog found himself perched atop a totally ginormous bunch of bananas. Before him, a few leather-winged bats were happily hanging upside down in the tree. A couple of them had unzipped a banana and were snacking away, while the others chattered away, saying things like, 'Remember that curve ball?' and 'Strike out, dude.' Sonic had no idea what they were talking about.

'Hi, blue dude', one of the bats greeted him. 'We're Baseball Bats. What are you?' Sonic groaned; what a pathetic joke!

'I'm Sonic the World-Famous Hedgehog,' he replied politely.

'Never heard of you, man. Who you pitch for? You played in the Mobius Series a long ways back or somethin'?' the bat said casually.

'Erm, not exactly,' the hedgehog said slowly. The bat saw his confusion at their odd speech and smirked.

'Huh, can't follow the lingo, huh, dude? You wanna try the next tree along if you want really weird.'

'What's there?' Sonic said, beginning to get irritable and fearing another feeble gag was looming on the comedy horizon.

'They're the Cricket Bats, man. They'll give you a load of stuff about googlies, losing your bails and getting caught in the gully. It'll make your eyes water just to listen, man.' The bat sniffed disdainfully.

Sonic wasn't perched increasingly precariously in the tree to hear any more of this. 'Look, dude, have you seen these new bats? They might have been heading to the Scrap Brain Zone?'

'Sure have, man,' the baseball bat replied. 'I tell you something, those guys won't be at zip in the fourth innings.'

'What does that mean?' Sonic pleaded.

'It means, man, that they're robots, yeah?' Sonic knew that and settled for looking impatient. But what the Baseball Bat went on to say was another kettle of bananas. 'And they nest in that weird-looking castle some dude just built on the hill, up in the Scrap Brain Zone.'

Sonic's eyes widened. A castle? In that place? Robotnik,

it had to be Robotnik . . . The hedgehog took a step back in amazement. Then he realised there weren't any bananas underneath him any more and he hit the ground hard.

'Bogus!' he lamented. 'Combing time for those super-cool spines again.'

Mickey just sniggered.

4

BRING ON THE EGGSTRAS

Sonic felt faintly guilty. He'd made his bestest buddy spend most of the day walking through muddy woods, looking for cold, hard, heavy lumps of metal, when he'd spent the time shooting the breeze and eating crisps and peanuts with Mickey. Apart from having to do a quick brush-up on his spines after the minor accident in the banana tree, he'd had an easy time of it. Now, heading back to the Green Hill Zone, he was looking forward to his pizza, fries and soda shake.

The vampire bat completely surprised him. Sonic was overwhelmed as the thing swooped on him from behind, its hard metal body forcing him to the ground. Sonic struggled desperately against the overbearing weight; he couldn't get his arms or legs free and the huge metal fangs of the monster were bearing down on his neck. He was helpless, and he realised to his utter horror that, at last, Robotnik was going to destroy him with one of his infernal creations!

'Woah! If only Tails were here!' he gasped.

'You called, chum?' The weight lifted.

Sonic spun around and upwards to find a twin-tailed fox with large chunks of robot armour tied to his body. He looked pretty puffed out, but horribly pleased with himself.

'I thought I would teach you a lesson,' Tails said crossly. 'I spent all day looking for all this junk. So I thought I'd put it to some use.'

'Phew, you had me scared there for a second,' Sonic said. Tails looked really pleased with himself'. 'Oh yeah, really scared. I might have used my Super-Super-Turbo-Super-Spinneroonie and kicked you right into orbit! Wow, I'm readily glad I didn't react too fast,' the hedgehog concluded, wiping a bead of imaginary sweat from his brow.

Now Tails looked scared. 'You mean, I might have ended up –'

'Let's not think about it, buddy,' Sonic said gravely, placing one concerned hand on his pal's shoulder. 'It's just too horrible. Come on.'

They walked along quietly for a while, before Tails said, 'But you don't have a Super-Super-Turbo-Spinneroonie manoeuvre!'

'And sometimes you don't have a brain,' sniggered Sonic. Tails had been very slow on the uptake.

They had a good laugh together. Then the fox clapped a paw to his head and lamented. 'Oh, maybe I don't! I forgot to tell you. These robot parts: they're from Robotnik!'

'Who else makes them?' Sonic pointed out.

'Well, according to that TV documentary exposé last week, about fifty different companies.'

'Yeah, well,' Sonic admitted defensively. 'Under contract to Robotnik, of course.'

'But here,' and with that Tails flourished a wing section, 'this miniature jet engine was built by Robotnik Aeronautics. Look at the mark.'

Sonic inspected the logo. 'Hmmm. Not as cool as mine,' he judged. 'Some people have no taste.'

'Some people think that fat Italian waiters are funny,' Tails pointed out. 'It's a funny old world, chummy.'

Sonic looked sideways at his friend, a puzzled expression on his heroic hedgehoggy face. 'Sorry, Sonic,' Tails apologised, 'it's something I heard Mickey say once. I don't know what it means.'

Sonic's eyes lit up. 'Ah, right on, dude! That reminds me I'd forgotten something as well. I met these bats down at Mickey's place and this is what they told me . . .'

Eggor checked through the listing for the film crew for the *Castle Robotnik* movie. His master had several crews of cameramen, second directors, key grips, and all those other people who exist only in order to get their names in the credits of a movie. Like everyone else on Mobius, and indeed on every other Tinseltown-fixated world throughout the vast ever-spinning universe, Eggor was finally faced with the Ultimate Unanswerable Question.

'What the heck is a Best Boy?' the robot pondered.

Eggor admired the special effects and the monsters Robotnik had assembled for the movie. He was checking through the stunts when Robotnik himself appeared after his breakfast. Frothy little dribbles of egg white hung on the underside of his enormous moustache. It was grosser than any special-effects unit could dream up.

'Ah, good robot! Checking the technical details. Well done, Eggor!' Robotnik was in a happy mood this morning.

'Thank you again, master.' Eggor had bypassed his Scientist-Flattering Circuit and gone straight to the Grovelling Program.

'Ah, but I see you have not yet eggsamined the monster list!' Robotnik cried, wobbling with pleasure. 'Look, Eggor!'

Eggor saw the full scope of Robotnik's genius. Once, he recalled, his Master had tried to imprison all Sonic's animal friends in robot form. Again, he had tried to actually turn

them into robots, or inanimate objects, or computer games. And this time . . .

'It is wonderful, master. Most splendid, truly – ' The robot stalled for a fraction of a second. It was the one in the bandages he didn't like too much, and he felt a stabbing pain in some distant circuit he couldn't immediately identify. 'Um, truly Mobius Prize-winningly worthy,' he concluded strangely ungrammatically.

A red light gleamed on the computer console before Eggor, distracting Robotnik from noticing the tiny glitch in Eggor's response. The lunatic trumpeted in delight.

'Ha ha-ha-hah! Our distant sensors have picked up the villains of the piece! Now our cast is complete! Come, Eggor, all we have to do now is to take the monorail and make our way to Castle Robotnik itself. There, we shall ascend the Great Tower and begin work on the climax of this work of genius! Ha ha ha ha ha!

'Eggor, we shall win Eggscars for this!'

'Eggscars, master? What are they?' This crucial piece of information was missing from the robot's memory banks. Robotnik scowled at him.

'Movie awards, Eggor. The MMA awards them every year for the best actor, best actress, best director, and so on. There's even an award for the person who offers them the biggest bribe every year.' Robotnik could see that Eggor was lost. 'The Mobius Movie Academy, Eggor; what else?'

'Ah,' the robot pondered, hastily downloading the relevant data from Robotnik's computers into his memory chips, 'is that the Mobius Movie Academy of which you are Life President, master?'

'Naturally,' Robotnik preened himself. 'And this year, I shall be presenting myself with the one Mobius Prize I have never won – in addition to all the Eggscars. And there will be an Eggscar for you too, good robot. Now, I have to program the Assistant Director, and then we shall make for the castle itself.'

Eggor didn't much like the look of the Assistant Director as it trundled in to the laboratory. Very implausibly for a metal robot, it had a very sharp suit, gleaming yellow-tinted shades and an unnerving gleam in its eyes.

'Hi, dude,' it said to Eggor. 'I'm a Spielbot. Pleased to meet you.'

'That's an odd name, isn't it?' Eggor replied rather haughtily.

'No way. I have a Mark III Robotnik Speak-Cool Emulator,' it sniffed. 'I can talk like, truly groovy. Yo! I can put the spiel on you and talk the hind legs off a robodonkey, dude. Hence, I'm a Spielbot.'

Eggor didn't like it. It was too brilliantly polished and too sure of itself.

'I have briefed all the eggstras, master,' the Spielbot informed Robotnik. The fat scientist wobbled with glee.

'Then all that is left is to finalise your programming,' Robotnik said. That can best be done in the castle itself. Come, my beautiful little Spielbot! Let us go and plan our acceptance speeches at the Eggscars ceremony!'

5

I USED TO BE A WEREWOLF BUT I'M ALL RIGHT NOW-OOOOOH!

It was yet another dark and stormy night; blimey, everyone was thinking, but Mobius has had a real run of bad weather lately.

The thunder was so loud that the noise shattered the metal remains of junked robots in Scrap Brain Zone. Oh all right, it wasn't really that loud; exaggerating like this is called 'poetic licence', or 'lying' to everyone else. But it was still SERIOUSLY NOISY! When bolts of lightning hit the ground, which they did constantly, they set fire to everything in a five-kilometre radius. Or they would have, if there hadn't also been raindrops the size of enormous inflated beach balls which splattered into the ground and extinguished the flames as soon as they took hold. The owls had long ago decided to migrate south for the winter, leaving behind only the few trees which hadn't pulled up their roots and done the same. Only a person who should have been certified as dangerously insane by the Mobius Psychiatric Institute for Total Nutters would even dream about setting foot outside on a night like this. Except for two radically cool superheroes, of course.

'Phew, Sonic, the line between being dangerously insane as defined by the Mobius Psychiatric Institute for Total Nutters and being a superhero is a very fine one,' Tails pondered as he dodged another enormous raindrop.

'Whassat?' enquired a very wet and miserable hedgehog. Porker Lewis's umbrella had been blown inside-out and ruined within a few seconds of Sonic holding it over his head, and now his spines were lying limply on his back and his sneakers were sodden. It was a serious bummer.

'Nothing,' Tails sighed. Suddenly, above the noise of the thunder and lightning, the night was disturbed by a plaintive and terrible cry.

'Oooooooooh-*ooooohhhhhh!*' it went plaintively.

Tails looked at Sonic with real fear in his eyes, and he gripped the tiny fragment of sodden garlic pizza firmly in his paws. By now, what with all the rain, the pizza had turned into a disgusting mush and it squeezed out through his paws on to the ground.

'There aren't any wolves in the Scrap Brain Zone,' Sonic sniffed derisively. 'Everyone knows that.'

'Oooooooooh-*ooooohhhhh,*' the cry came again, this time much nearer.

'Do you want to tell him that? Tails said, shrinking back in fear. 'Look, I know a bit about wolves. I am a fox, after all. They're like us, only much, much bigger. And I know for a fact that they eat hedgehogs.'

'No they don't. They eat pizza like everyone else does.'

'Well, all right, so I'm not certain that they eat hedgehogs,' Tails said defensively. He had felt scared, and a bit ashamed of being the only one who was frightened, so he'd hoped to make Sonic feel a bit like he did. 'But I don't think they eat pizza either. And they do

have really big jaws, dripping with drool, and they're big enough to rip – '

'OK, like, chill out,' Sonic snapped. 'That's enough. It's probably just a noise Robotnik is have played over some loudspeakers on the castle walls or something.'

Suddenly, there was a break in the black clouds scudding across the sky, and they could see a yellow full moon glaring balefully down at them. They heard the wailing sound again, this time much, much louder and much, much closer. Lightning crackled and the scene was suddenly illuminated in garish blue. Only a few metres away from the pair stood a totally humungously huge wolf. Its fur was grey and flecked with silver and it had an enormous pair of jaws. They were wide open, and it licked its lips as it looked at Tails and Sonic. It had that look that wolves only have when they haven't eaten for a long time and when they've just seen something really, really juicy. But the weirdest thing about it was that it had two tails!

Tails hid behind Sonic and peered out over his shoulder, his eyes as wide as a pair of family-sized deep pan pizzas.

'Yikes!' he whimpered. 'What are we going to do?'

'I said chill out,' Sonic replied nervously. 'Maybe we can talk to it.' Shouting to make himself heard to the wolf over the sound of thunder and lightning, he yelled out, 'Like hi, there, wolf-dude, which way to the castle?'

'Yum, yum!' replied the wolf, licking its lips and padding a bit closer to them. It sniffed the air hopefully.

'Oh, like, you don't want to eat us,' Sonic said as he backed away a little. 'I mean, I'm covered in really grody spines. They'd stick in your throat. And my buddy here, well, he's a fox, so eating him would almost be cannibalism, you know? And that's just really gross, man.'

'We saw this little girl in a red cloak and hood a bit further down the road,' Tails lied. 'She was carrying a really neat basket of stuff. Ever so good to eat!' Sonic looked at him disapprovingly. 'I meant what was in the basket, not the little girl, of course,' Tails said defensively. 'Though maybe her granny is edible.'

The wolf walked up to them and stuck a very wet snout into Sonic's chest. He looked vaguely disappointed.

'Now look, you're not playing fair, you know,' the wolf said testily. 'You're supposed to run around screaming and terrified and all that kind of carry-on.'

'Why?' Sonic enquired.

'Because it's in the script, that's why.' Before Sonic could ask what the wolf meant, it jerked back its shaggy head and howled again.

'Oh man, like, turn down your volume; you're giving me a headache,' Sonic complained, holding his paws over his ears. The wolf looked really bummed that his howl hadn't terrified Sonic witless.

'What's this script?' Tails asked.

'You don't need to know any details, you can improvise,' the wolf said airily, 'but you're going to have to run around some. After all, I *am* a werewolf. Come on guys, get into it a bit more. Let's have some real feeling!'

'Why have you got two tails?' Sonic enquired.

'That's not important right now. Just run around and scream a bit!'

'Not until you've told us how come you have two tails like my buddy here,' Sonic insisted.

'Weeelllll', the wolf said slowly, playing for time, 'I really think you'd have to speak to someone in make-up or maybe the special effects department about that, to be honest. Now, are you guys going to run around a bit or do I have to get really nasty?' It opened its jaws so wide they could see its tonsils. Its teeth were very, very large and it seemed to have more of them than wolves usually do, but when you're just about to get eaten by one it's probably a bit tricky to count all the teeth to be absolutely sure about this.

'You know, Mr Wolf, you're forgetting one vital thing. I have, hidden in my coat, a musket with a silver bullet,' Tails fibbed. The wolf backed off a little.

'You're bluffing,' it said.

'You can't be certain of that,' Tails said evenly just like he'd seen them do countless times on the telly. The wolf stood its ground and considered its options.

'Well, look, how about this,' it offered. 'You're going to the castle, right? Well, if I tell you how to get into it, will you at least run there so I can chase you a bit and look good? This is my big scene, after all. If I make good in this my agent says I could get my own spin-off mini-series.'

'Okay, dude, seems reasonable to me,' Sonic said. It didn't really seem reasonable at all, because he didn't have the faintest idea of what was going on, what with all this nonsense about scripts, scenes and agents. And there was still one thing he badly wanted to get straight. 'But only if you tell us why you have two tails.'

'Well,' the wolf whispered conspiratorially, 'this is a secret, but I guess I can let you in on it. The Producer designed me this way.'

'Designed you?' Sonic wondered. 'Are you one of Robotnik's robots? Because if you are – '

'No way! Whoever told you that was lying,' the wolf said hurriedly. 'I'm an organic construct,' it added proudly. 'And as a matter of fact, I'm based on him.' It pointed one of its huge paws at Tails. 'The Producer is basing his cast on, um, erm, biological timeplates.' It clearly wasn't sure that it had got that part exactly right. 'Look, I'm not sure that I got that part exactly right. Don't quote me.'

'This is weird,' Tails muttered in Sonic's ear. 'Robotnik's up to something. What is it this time?'

'Dunno, buddy, but as usual there's only one way to find out,' Sonic grimaced. He was tapping one fashionably sneakered foot on the ground now, plainly impatient with all this talk.

'Getting ready to run a bit?' the wolf said hopefully. 'Come on guys, give me a break. The castle is only half a kilometre away. Just go left past the pile of junked Buzzers and turn sharp right at the heap of rusted Turtloids and you can't miss it. There's a secret way in through the castle vaults just to the left of the main gates. You could go in through the gates, of course, but that's much more dangerous.'

'Gee, thank you,' Tails smiled and twirled his tails a bit to shake the rainwater off them. The wolf noticed him and did the same, covering everyone in a great spray of water.

'Hmmm. I think my tails are a bit bigger than yours,' he said mournfully to the saturated hedgehog and fox. 'Right, let's get going. Try to, well, scream a bit convincingly too, okay? Ready? Action!'

They rushed off through the Scrap Brain Zone, Tails giving the occasional frightened squeak and the great wolf keeping pace behind them, snarling a lot and howling occasionally.

'What's old Fat and Eggy up to this time?' Tails gasped between puffs of breath as they raced along. 'He's tried to trap all the animals inside robots, then he tried to change them into robots, and now he's making his own monsters out of us all! I don't want to be a werefox!'

'Fret not, little buddy,' Sonic growled. 'We're going to put a stop to this nonsense once and for all!'

They saw the wide open, rusty gates to the castle vault looming out of the falling rain right before them. Sonic kicked the gates off their hinges just for the heck of it and they raced inside, leaving only the yellow glowing eyes of the werewolf gleaming happily in the darkness behind them.

It was dark in the vault and they didn't spot the trap in the

floor. When they stepped on to it, great metal plates swung open and they dropped straight down into darkness even blacker than the night outside. They hit the floor with a thump and heard the sound of crunching metal as the plates of the pit trap sealed themselves shut over their heads. Sonic and Tails were trapped in Castle Robotnik!

6

WE'RE OFF TO SEE THE WIZARD

'Eugh, it's a bit smelly down here,' Tails complained. 'This must be where pizzas which go past their sell-by date come to die.'

Sonic was trying to see where they were. The floors and walls were made of brickwork and there were burning torches stuck into metal rings in the walls in the distance. There was just enough light to see by, but all he could see was a passage extending quite some way into the distance, and only one way to go. He didn't like the idea of being in a dead-end one little bit.

'I don't like the idea of being in a dead-end one little bit,' Sonic confirmed. 'I can take a run-up and smash our way out of here,' he said, looking up to where the overhead metal plates were. It was too dim, where he stood, for him to actually see them.

'Why don't we just explore a bit? Let's see where this goes,' Tails suggested. 'The wolf said this was a safer way in. I think I trust him. A bit.'

'You can't trust animals just because they have two

tails,' Sonic said. 'But okay, it's your call. So, like, let's get on with it.'

They padded forward along the gloomy passageway. Before long, they were up to their knees in gunky dark water and that smelled horrible too.

'Yuck,' Tails complained. 'This is like the polluted parts of the Aquatic Ruin Zone. Where that Robotnik's been up to his dastardly tricks.'

'Ssshhh! I think I heard something,' Sonic said. He was really narked by now, because his sneakers were going to be ruined if he had to go on treading water much longer.

'Do you hear anything unusual–?' His question was cut off just before he could finish it. Behind them, there was an ominous crunching noise of moving stone, and from a secret wall in the passage three very weird-looking chickens emerged. They looked vaguely like their friend Chirps, but there was something very wrong about the way they moved and they smelled really, really, really bad. As the pair spun to face them, exactly the same noise came from in front of them, and another hidden door in the wall opened. Another group of these weird-looking chickens walked slowly out into the passage.

'Pooh! Those chickens need deodorants,' Tails said in disgust as the creatures lumbered slowly towards them. 'Look! They've got bits hanging off them! And their feathers are really shabby and filthy! Oh Blimey! Sonic, they're zombies! Look at their wild staring eyes and 'orrible bodies! I've seen them in videos! We can't stop them! They're undead! The horror! The horr – '

'Nonsense!' Sonic interrupted sniffily. 'Totally bogus. Whoever heard of zombie chickens? They're just some new kind of robot, and that means we can bounce them! Yee haw!' The hedgehog whirled around, spun some and launched himself at the nearest creature.

It was gross-out city, folks. When the whirling hedgehog

struck the nearest zombie chicken, well, quite a lot of it fell apart. Big gobbets of rotting chicken splattered the walls everywhere. You don't want to know the details; well, all right, maybe you do, but let's just say that it was utterly disgusting! Sonic looked terrible, like he'd been for a quick spin around the butcher's tray. He was covered in icky feathers and less identifiable, erm, stuff. But at least he knew the chickens weren't robots. They really did seem to be zombie chickens.

The creatures lurched even closer, further towards them, their beaks clucking insanely, driving at Sonic and Tails to peck them to pieces. Even the one with an awful lot of its body missing just kept right on moving at them. Terror-stricken, the two animals managed to duck between the legs of the zombies and run ahead, into the depths of the castle. They hadn't got very far at all when a new group of humans loomed out of the gloom up ahead of them in the distance.

'Oh no! More zombies!' Tails whimpered.

'Zombies? Did you say Zombies?' said one of the advancing people in a very strange voice. It sounded like he was talking through his nose. 'Gadzooks, Gentle Adventurers, the forces of darkness lie before us! Our greatest challenge awaits! Saddle my destrier – er, well, perhaps not.'

'Huh, Zombies,' sniffed another of the humans. 'Only two ruddy hit dice. Pushover. Bet they won't have any treasure. Why don't we shoot the Dark Elf scene again?'

'Who are these dweebs, and more to the point, what on Mobius are they talking about? Are they mad?' Tails wondered aloud. 'I don't think we ought to tell them those things we left behind are zombie chickens, though,' he added in a quiet sideways whisper to Sonic.

'Nay, Gentle Creatures of the Forests, we are not mad,' said the man. 'Though brave Drizzle here was once

affected in his mind by a powerful magical curse by a foul servant of the Dark Lord!'

'Yeah, I remember that,' came a woman's voice. 'Dead scary that was. Gazza the Dark Lord, I ask you! I hate these low-budget jobs with tacky scriptwriters.'

They could see the four people now. The man with the very silly voice looked almost like a robot. He was dressed all over in funny metal plates, and carried a shield in one hand and a sword in the other. Beside him stood an enormous brute of a man, wearing just a few furs and carrying a great two-handed axe. He had muscles in places where most people don't have places, but he didn't half look cold. Behind them, a thin and stooping man in a long dark cloak with funny symbols all over it wore a pointed hat and kept picking at his fingernails. To one side stood the woman, who wore various flimsy garments made out of leather which were obviously two sizes too small for her. It was plain that she was rather chilly too.

'What are you?' Tails asked rather impolitely.

'Well, Gentle Creature, I am Sir Norbert the Paladin,' the metal man said proudly. 'Doubtless, bards have sung my fame in the small and backward settlement from which you hail. I am a slayer of Dragons, feller of Giants, a servant of the Powers of Light, foe of the Forces of Darkness, and – '

'Yes, all right Nobby, don't go on about it, they'll get bored,' the woman said rather irritably. 'They're only extras, anyway. The real scene is with the Zombies, so I suppose we'd better get on with it. I'll stand around and gasp and breathe heavily and be totally useless in a stereotyped way while you and Thug chop them up and Drizzle casts some flashy spell special effects will tart up later. It's so boring.'

'Thug?' Sonic asked. It didn't sound very pleasant.

'I yam Thug the Barbarian,' the brute with the axe said in a strangely accented monotone, slapping his chest with a ham-sized fist. 'Hasta la vista, hedgehog!'

'No, Thug,' the woman said very patiently, 'that was in that other movie, all those years ago before you became a washed-up has-been.' Thug looked slightly perplexed and repeated his line. The woman shook her head slightly. 'It's the only thing he can remember these days. It's all very sad,' she said by way of explanation.

'We need a Dwarf down here,' the man in the cloak said off-handedly. 'Or a Gnome, but they're harder for make-up to get right. Dwarfs are really good in these underground passages. Are either of you Dwarfs?'

'Don't be so thick, Drizzle. Wizards are supposed to be intelligent,' the woman sighed. 'Of course they're not Dwarves. The budget wouldn't run to one.'

'Well, thanks be to you, small random-encounter Gentle Creatures,' the metal man said in a patronizing tone of voice. 'Now we must sally forth and I shall use my holy banishing powers against the undead denizens of these dark and infernal depths.'

'He is mad, whatever he says. Absolutely barking,' Tails whispered to Sonic, surreptitiously tapping the side of his forehead with one finger.

The hedgehog was truly baffled. He knew where he stood with robots; he could spin and leap and bounce and deal with them, but all this demons and dungeons stuff was confusing him a lot. Sonic didn't like being confused, because then he had to think and that made his brain hurt.

'I suppose I'll have to use the Ebon Staff of Peaminster the Magnificent?' Drizzle said hopefully. 'I look really good in that kind of scene, you know. All that underlighting makes me look really cool and awesomely macho and powerful.' He flexed his non-existent biceps. The woman groaned quietly to herself.

Sonic drew her aside and whispered to her. 'Look, um,

you seem to be the only one with any brains here,' he began hopefully.

'Don't I know it, luvvie. And I get cast as Bimbette the thief! Typical low-budget stereotyped rubbish,' she complained bitterly.

'Well, like, do you know how to get into the main castle from here?' Sonic enquired.

'Just a minute, I'll check on our dungeon map,' she said kindly.

At that moment, from out of the darkness, a very peculiar-looking robot clanked up to the group. It unfolded a canvas-backed chair with the words *Assistant to the Assistant Director* painted on the back and plonked it down before the scene. It looked vaguely like an Octus, and its many robotic arms held a variety of clipboards, mini-cameras and other oddities. It sat itself down in the chair, folding a few legs underneath itself, and began to give orders.

'Look, luvvies, wrong film, I'm afraid,' it said patiently to the people. 'We're way over budget and the producer has decided to junk the movie. Terribly sorry, luvs, but that's showbiz. You know how it is.' The four people all looked extremely surprised and disgruntled.

'You can't do this!' Sir Norbert complained. 'I haven't had my great dragon-slaying scene yet!'

'Hasta la vista, punk,' Thug growled, advancing on the alarmed robot with his axe raised.

'Now look, luvs, let's be reasonable, shall we?' the robot pleaded, waving several arms about in appeasement. 'You'll all be offered parts in future projects. Emma and Kenny baby, the producer wants you for the leads in *Boring Dweebs from the Planet Ego* next month, honestly.'

'Hey Sonic, why don't we just sneak away and leave them to it?' Tails begged his companion.

'Not a bad idea,' grumbled the hedgehog. He wanted to

bounce the robot and smash it to smithereens, but he wasn't sure how the people would react. They seemed to be getting very angry.

The two friends began to creep away from the furiously arguing robot and people. They were almost out of sight when the man in the cloak spotted them.

'Oi! There they go! It's their fault. They want to be bigger stars than us and they've persuaded the producer to cut our contracts!' he yelled furiously. 'Let's get 'em.'

'That would be morally wrong,' Sir Norbert said pompously.

'Shut up Nobby, you're the only good guy around here. Have a dose of the Ebon Staff of Peaminster, you suckers!' The cloaked man raised a long stick and pointed it at Tails and Sonic. They ducked and ran. Behind them, clanking metal and yelling voices told them the humans were in hot pursuit.

They kept on running. They didn't have any idea what the Ebon Staff of Peaminster the Magnificent might do until a huge spout of flame shot across their heads four metres ahead into the distance.

'Yikes!' Tails exclaimed. 'We have got to get out of here – '

Then they saw the zombies ahead of them. They were just standing around, doing nothing, passing the time just like all undead chickens do, but when they saw Tails and Sonic they lurched into action. The heroes were trapped between the zombies and the pursuing humans.

'Hey! Big scene time!' Sonic yelled. Finally, he'd realised what must be going on here. 'Forces of Darkness right ahead this way! Like, really heinous Undead Things from the Powers of Darkness right here!' He'd even got his head around all that Talking in Capitals nonsense.

'I hear thee, Good Creature!' came Sir Norbert's plummy voice. The friends stood aside as the humans charged past

and raced at the zombies. Letting them go by, Tails and
Sonic immediately shot off in the opposite direction.

'Aren't they going to be really disappointed when they
find out that they're chickens?' Tails said anxiously.

'We'll be far enough away by then,' Sonic replied. Then
he explained his insight to his foxy friend.

'It's so obvious when you think about it: Robotnik's
making a movie,' Sonic said. 'It's the only thing that makes
sense out of this. All that bogus nonsense about scripts
and contracts. Oh, and the producer: that's just got to be
Robotnik.'

'There's got to be more to it than that,' Tails said, puffed
a little.

'Oh yeah, like, obviously,' Sonic said, a trifle annoyed
because he'd thought that he'd worked it all out. He didn't
know what more there was, but he was determined to find
out.

The two of them were so busy racing along the passages
to get away from the fracas behind them that they ran right
into another trap. All along the passage, behind and in front
of them, great metal pendulums suddenly descended from
the ceiling. At the ends of the pendulums were razor-sharp
curved blades, and as the pendulums swung to and fro
they came lower and lower, scything through the air just
above their heads.

'Oh no! We're going to be slice-and-dice!' Tails moaned.

'No way! The only thing that gets sliced around here is
the pepperoni for our next snack,' Sonic snarled heroically.
Revving himself up to full pelt, he shot off in a blaze of
whirring red sneakers. Behind him, two tails turned into
propellers and a fox buzzed along just above ground level.

They hurtled right into a dead end. Ahead of them, they
could see two horrible metal objects. One was hedgehog-
shaped and one was fox-shaped. They were great metal
shells filled with spikes. They were hinged and it was clear

that if they were shut there would just be room to fit Tails and Sonic inside – with all the spikes inside them! Tails shivered in revulsion.

'I've seen them in horror movies,' the fox shuddered. 'It's a, what is it, erm, Iron Maiden?'

'This is no time to talk about heinously bogus music!' Sonic complained. 'We've got to get out of here, dude.' There was no way back as a hundred pendulums swung barely a centimetre above the ground in the passageway beyond. The hedgehog looked around for any possible means of escape. Above him, maniacal laughter boomed around the dank and dirty chamber.

'Welcome! Ha ha ha! Welcome to Castle Robotnik! Welcome to my nightmare, hedgehog. Ha ha ha!'

'What are you trying this time, most heinous deranged mad genius-type lunatic?' Sonic bellowed, with just a touch of overkill.

'You will see, you will see! Spielbot, work the camera around for a close-up on the fox, he looks really scared,' Robotnik gloated. Above them, they could see a wall-mounted camera swivelling and a zoom lens shoot forward. Angrily, Sonic whirled into a Super Spin, shot upwards, and bounced the camera into a pile of useless junk.

'You blue menace! You'll pay for this!' Robotnik's furious voice screamed from the hidden loudspeaker. 'You'll never get out alive! You're doomed, I said, doomed. Ha ha ha!'

Sonic, however, had seen the crack in the wall close to where he had smashed the camera. With another prodigious leap, he launched himself at it. He saw stars after the impact and whirled unsteadily back to the ground, but now he could see a hole smashed in the wall; rainwater was dripping in from high above. This must be a way out of the castle dungeons!

Sonic and Tails flew upwards leaving the enraged screams of the mad Dr Robotnik behind them. They managed to get their paws anchored on the wet earth at the top of the chute and haul themselves back into the night. A sudden flash of lightning high above them revealed the gates of Castle Robotnik in the near distance and, as they stared at the gothic wrought-iron of the gates, they silently opened. Rushing down the drive from the castle, the whinnying of frightened horses and the cracking of whips advancing before it, came a black carriage with a ghostly rider atop it. Maniacal laughter trailed in its wake.

'Here we go again,' Sonic grumbled. 'And not even time for a take five-type snack break between scenes!'

7

THE BUTLER DID IT!

Sonic and Tails barely leapt out of the way of the madly careering carriage in time. By now, they weren't in the slightest bit surprised to see a Headless Horseman driving the carriage on into the raging storm.

'I wasn't surprised to see a Headless Horseman driving that carriage into the raging storm.' Tails said helpfully. 'I suppose it's some kind of special effect.'

'Yeah,' Sonic said coolly, 'but that wasn't what was really radically spooky about it.'

'What was really radically spooky about it, then?' Tails asked.

'The horses didn't have any heads either.'

'Oh.' Tails gave a little noise, like a small, frightened fox giving a small, frightened gulp.

As they approached the open gates, Tails had a brainwave of his own.

'Sonic, I think I know what Robotnik's doing apart from making a movie,' he said. Sonic looked interested. 'Think about it. We've met a werewolf that looked a bit like me,

and zombie chickens that looked like Chirps. Robotnik's making us into horror film monsters!'

Sonic looked disgruntled. Thinking about complicated concepts like that didn't please him. He felt much better doing things like smashing Robotnik's cameras, so he distracted himself a few moments by bouncing on top of the two mounted on top of the castle gates. Satisfied by that, and tucking into a pack of barbecue crisps he'd found in one pocket so fast that they didn't even get a tiny little bit soggy in the driving rain, he let Tails continue.

'I suppose it's the next thing for him to try,' Tails offered. 'Remember, he's failed in trying to imprison us in robotic Prison Eggs, failed to turn us into robots, failed to turn us into kitchen utensils, failed to ensure we never existed and failed to infect us with computer viruses,' Tails said, handily summing up all of their adventures to date. 'Now he's going to turn us into video-style monsters! Another of his eggsperi– sorry, I mean, experiments.'

'I suppose it makes a crazy kind of sense,' Sonic said doubtfully. He couldn't see why Robotnik would go to such lengths. He didn't know about the Mobius Prize Robotnik wanted to win, and he certainly didn't know what Robotnik was building in the great tower atop the castle. Whoops! Erm, forget we mentioned that.

'Oh no!' Tails clasped his paws over his eyes. 'Think – Porker's already been bitten by a vampire bat! Perhaps there was something in the bat's bite which may be turning Porker into a monster right now! Some heinous substance from the Chemical Plant Zone or something. Sonic, we've got to move fast!'

'Yeah, let's go!' Sonic agreed.

They shot off up the drive and stood before the great wooden doors of the castle. They could see that it was really huge; well, after all, it did have five towers and high stone walls. As they tried to take in just how big it was, the wooden front doors creaked open. Before them stood a penguin in a tuxedo with long flowing black coat-tails. He was very tall, very thin, and very pale indeed.

'Good evening, gentlemen,' the penguin said in a really slimy voice. 'The Count is expecting you for dinner.'

'Yikes!' Tails exclaimed to Sonic. 'The werewolf was going to eat us, and now – '

'No, persons of savagely limited intelligence,' the penguin said smoothly. 'You are to take dinner with the Count. He has so few visitors these days. He will be very glad to have company.'

'Why should we want to have dinner with this bogus dude?' Sonic said suspiciously. He wanted to stomp the butler, but the similarity to Tux was a bit disconcerting.

'Because I make the finest pizza on all of Mobius,' the penguin said, raising its eyebrows slightly. 'With every topping you request and beautifully melted cheese, bubbling and browned to a degree of absolute perfection, with a tray of different relishes, ketchups and – '

Sonic was finding it hard to speak, because he was drooling so much. Okay, well, like, let's see this Count dude,' he slobbered. 'Go heavy on the sweetcorn and easy on the peppers okay?'

'As you wish, sir,' the penguin said. 'Please walk this way.' He strolled casually into the gloomy hall of the castle.

The fox sniggered and said to Sonic, 'I'd rather not. He walks kinda funny.'

Sonic glowered. 'Come on, buddy, this is a time for better jokes than that.'

'I think we ought to try to take a look around to see what we're up against,' Tails whispered to Sonic as they padded along behind the penguin. 'Then we can smash it up.' He knew Sonic's first instinct would be to bounce anything and everything in sight, but Tails wanted to know what they were getting themselves into before getting too radically

aggressive. Sonic usually needed to be carefully persuaded of the wisdom of such caution. For his part, the
hedgehog merely grunted and continued to glower.

'We also have to find out exactly what Robotnik is up to
before we smash it up. We may have to find some kind of
cure for Porker if he's turning into a vampire,' Tails added in
a whisper. Reluctantly, Sonic agreed, even though he
didn't really think that Porker was in any danger.

'Excuse me, tall, dark and uninteresting, I don't think I
caught your name,' Tails said to the penguin, catching up
to his shoulder.

'I am Ferdy, the Count's butler,' the penguin said very
smoothly as he walked on.

'Ferdy? Isn't that a funny name for a penguin?' Tails
asked.

'Well, sir, if you ask me Tails is a pretty dumb name for a
fox. It shows that your parents had no imagination,' the
penguin replied in a superior tone of voice.

'Oh, that's not my real name, it's just a nickname everyone calls me by,' Tails informed him. 'Do you have a
nickname?'

'Certainly not,' the penguin retorted, sounded slightly
offended. 'A gentleman's gentleman such as myself would
never have an appellation so vulgarly common.

'Oooh! Pardon me for existing, I'm sure,' Tails said
rather crossly. He slouched back and rejoined Sonic, who
was taking in the decor as they crossed the immense
hallway.

'Look at all this,' the hedgehog snarled. 'Totally bogus.
Suits of armour and shields and heraldry and all that boring
old stuff. I bet those suits of armour are robots. And there's
only one way to find that out, dude.' He whirled and spun
and flew into the nearest suit of armour, stood up against a
wall. When he'd finished demolishing it, he discovered that
it was just a suit of armour after all.

'Would you gentlemen kindly mind not behaving like total hooligans?' the butler said with a steely edge beneath his ever-polite tone of voice. Sonic was beginning to dislike this penguin intensely, but he also felt very sheepish.

'Uh, like, most radically sorry, domestic-servant-type guy,' he said. 'I just thought, like, that maybe someone was hiding in there. Spying on the Count, you know. You can't be too careful these days.'

'If anyone was spying on the Count, I'd know about it, sir,' the penguin replied frostily, and there was an evil glint in his deep, brown eyes. 'Now, would you care to have some entrées served in the guest lounge prior to dining?'

Tails had no idea what the butler meant, but he said yes anyway. He guessed that Ferdy would go away to fetch the entrées, whatever they were, and then he and Sonic could do a little private snooping.

'Wow, like fab to the max, this is great!' Tails enthused as they were ushered into a very comfortable room. The chairs were huge, and covered in soft cushions, and there was a massive video and games console. The fox's tails were twitching already.

'Would sirs care for a selection of nachos, crisps, nuts and cola?' the butler said: it was plain that he had been briefed on his guests' culinary favourites.

'Well, thanks dude, don't mind if we do,' Sonic said breezily. He was looking for hidden cameras. He guessed there must be one in the console and he was working himself up to bouncing it. The penguin retired to the lounge doorway, bowed stiffly, and closed the doors behind him as he left. Sonic bounced the console. It fell apart, but there weren't any cameras inside it.

'Hey, cool, buddy, I thought we were going to look around this place,' Tails said. 'I mean, can't we at least get the pizza before we smash anything up? I work better on a full stomach.'

'This Count,' Sonic growled, 'it's got to be Robotnik. He's going to try to destroy us again. It's a trap, I know it.'

'Maybe it isn't,' Tails said slowly. He was trying to think. Here it came. 'A Count – maybe he's a vampire! Oh no!'

'Look, you foolish fox, vampires don't really exist! It's all a plot by Robotnik,' Sonic said crossly.

'That's what Porker said, and look what happened to him. I hope Sally's putting fresh garlic round his neck every day like she said she would,' the fox said anxiously. Any further reply from Sonic was cut off as the lounge doors opened and the tall, thin penguin strolled in with a silver tray piled high with snacks.

'Please be so good as to ring the bell for service should you require it,' the penguin sleazed, bowing again. 'Dinner will be served at eight o'clock sharp.'

'Is there, like, somewhere where I can freshen myself up before dinner?' Sonic asked, not sure that he was really saying this. It was getting a little too weird for him. The butler, however, gave a beaming, beaky smile.

'Most certainly. I have in mind that sir might wish to brush his spines and, er, clean his rather disreputable-looking footwear?' Sonic looked sheepish. 'Well, sir, guest rooms have been prepared for you in the Blue Tower.'

'I bet they have,' Sonic muttered. The butler pretended not to have heard him.

'If you would be so good as to follow me, I will serve you your entrées in your guest suite,' the penguin offered. Tails thought he was very persuasive. Sonic thought he was an oily sleazeball.

'Just through here, sir,' the butler smarmed as he led them past the lounge and up the stairs to a small doorway with a curved arch atop it. 'Up the staircase and first on your left. There is a service bell should you require – '

'Yes, thank-you, captain beaky,' Sonic interrupted him rudely, grabbing the tray of goodies. 'See you for dinner, dude.' The penguin walked sedately off down the corridor. Sonic hurtled up the stairs and knocked down the door, which was tough to do without spilling the nuts everywhere, but he managed it.

'Crikey, this is superfabuloso!' Tails said delightedly. 'Look! Real four-poster beds, wow!' Tails just had to have a bounce. 'And those big windows with the funny drapes just like you get in, er . . .'

'Just like you get in vampire movies,.' Sonic teased him. 'And there aren't any mirrors in here either. Bogus or what?'

'So we can't tell if the Count is a vampire by checking to see if he has a reflection in a mirror!' Tails squeaked.

'No, you dweeb. I can't see how cool my spines look when I've finished combing them,' the hedgehog retorted.

Eggor was getting confused. Robotnik had changed his mind and wouldn't show him his Grand Eggsperiment on the top floor of the great tower. Robotnik had clearly been making another movie, because there was another robot film crew somewhere in the castle, and Eggor had to make a whole bunch of sensor scans to track them down. He reviewed their commands from the computer, and realized that they didn't seem to have anything to do now that Robotnik had abandoned his *Dungeons & Dweebs*™ movie project in favour of *Castle Robotnik*.

Eggor didn't like that smarmy Spielbot. He was jealous, or at least he would have been if he had had Emotion Circuits built into him. That Spielbot talked too smoothly and seemed too sure of itself. What's more, it was giving all the commands to the film crews. Eggor had already seen the script for his own part in the final scene for Robotnik's movie, and he wanteḍ to make absolutely sure that he looked really good in it. He didn't trust Spielbot to make him look that good.

An idea began to form in Eggor's brain. Since the first film crew has nothing to do, the master would surely want them to occupy their time usefully, he thought. And master says he will be very, very busy with his Great Eggsperiment. I would be being very helpful, and a really good robot, if I saved him the time of bothering with them, wouldn't I? Of course I would.

With a thin metallic smile hovering around his face, Eggor began to program the computer.

8

DINNER WITH A VAMPIRE

'Oh, wow! Fandabidozee!' Tails was over-excited. He'd found a brand-new dinner suit in the wardrobe of their guest suite, and he thought he looked really cool in it. Sonic didn't have the heart to point out that, with his two white-tipped tails poking out at the back, the fox looked faintly ridiculous.

'I'm sure you should dress formally for dinner as well,' he teased Sonic. The hedgehog just laughed.

'My sneakers are clean now and my spines are totally splendiferous, and that's smarter than anything on Mobius,' he said.

There was a gentle knock at the door to the guest rooms, which opened to reveal the butler.

'The Count awaits the pleasure of your company for dinner,' smarmed the penguin, and then retreated back outside.

'Like, where did he learn to speak like that?' Sonic pondered. 'It's just grody. If he was any more slimy he'd be a slug. And I'm not speaking monkey rhyming slang either.'

They opened the door slowly and looked carefully down the stone spiral staircase, expecting traps to come down from the ceiling at any moment. But, despite their fears, they made the little door at the bottom safely and skipped along to the lounge. Ferdy the butler was waiting.

'The dining hall is just along there to your right,' he said helpfully, pointing the way. 'May I humbly wish you a pleasant dining experience?'

'What a dweeb,' Sonic said in annoyance as they left the butler behind. He couldn't really get cross, though. His nose was already twitching at the wonderful smell of pizza coming from up ahead.

The hedgehog raced into the feast hall with a fox determined not to be done out of his fair share right behind him. The hall was vast, fitted with one of those wooden tables that go on for ever. Sonic reckoned he could have sat a hundred of his chums around it, but he was glad they weren't here. There wasn't enough pizza for that many.

There was silver cutlery, bone china plates, salvers, candlesticks, ornamental shields on the wall, crossed swords over the fireplace and – well, Sonic didn't care about any of that stuff. Forgetting his manners, he just launched himself at the nearest metre-diameter pizza. It was sweetcorn, tuna and anchovy, with mozzarella as thick as the deep pile carpet on the floor, and it tasted totally wonderful. He hadn't realized until now how famished he was. He slurped up slices of the pizza like, well, like a hungry vampire in a blood bank.

'I see zat you are enjoying yourselves,' a deep bass voice came booming from beside the huge black curtains covering the windows at the far end of the hall. They looked up, tomato paste smeared all over their mouths, to take in the hulking, cloaked figure swathed in darkness. Tails shrank back into a chair at the end of the table furthest away from the creature, and realized as he looked around that the doors to the feast hall had been closed. He gave a little squeak of fear, but Sonic didn't seem to be fazed at all.

'Greetings, Count-dude,' the hedgehog said casually as he carved up a slice of the pepperoni pizza next in line. 'Your butler really knows how to, er, buttle. This is groovy pizza, dude.'

'He has been with me for a long time,' the cloaked figure said mysteriously. It advanced forward into the half-light from the fire and small lamps in the hall. Then even Sonic shrank backwards.

The Count looked awfully like Joe Sushi. They'd never seen a walrus in full dinner jacket and coat-tails before, and he did look kind of strange with his flippers poking out of his jacket sleeves, but there was no mistaking the similarity. The eyes of the Count glowed a weird, hypnotic red, and his face was even paler than Ferdy's. His black cloak, lined with fine red silk, billowed out behind him.

'Pray sit and eat,' the weird creature invited them. 'It is being so rare zat I haff company.'

'Yeah, Ferdy-dude told us,' Sonic said. At that very moment, as if he had been waiting for his cue, the butler emerged carrying a large silver tray with a decanter of red wine and a single glass. He placed it before the Count as the latter sat his large, walrussy form down at the head of the table.

'Manners, Ferdy,' the Count reprimanded gently. 'Perhaps our guests vould be caring for a glass also.'

'No thanks, your Countship,' Sonic declined. 'Wine makes me feel kind of, well, sick actually. I'll stick to the fizzy stuff.'

The Count laughed as the butler quietly padded away. 'Vine! Ah, you are making such jokes, you hedgehogs.' He poured himself a glass of the thick red liquid.

Tails had a horrid suspicion, but decided to keep it to himself, at least for the time being. 'Have you lived here,

like, a long time, Mr Count?' he asked politely. He just wanted to learn everything he could, and then get out of here. The Count's glowing red eyes were very disturbing and the fox was extremely uncomfortable.

'Indeed. My family haff lived here for centuries,' the Count replied.

Sonic wondered what on Mobius was going on. He knew the castle couldn't have been here for more than a month or two, because he had made one of his rare forays into the Scrap Brain Zone not long ago and there hadn't been any sign of the place then. He didn't know whether to stomp the Count, run for the door or what; but the pizza was great and he wanted to eat a lot more before making any hasty decisions he might regret come dinner time.

'Oh, um, that's triffically interesting,' said Tails rather hopelessly. He was scared now and all Sonic was doing was stuffing his face with pizza.

'Ahhhh,' the Count sighed as he drained his glass, 'AB negative, and such a lovely vintage too. I only vish I had more in ze cellar.'

'The cellar?' Tails said, perking up. 'Where is that, exactly?'

The Count laughed evilly. 'Now, my friends, you cannot expect me to tell you zat. Because zen you vould find my coffins and destroy zem!'

Suddenly, the Count stood bolt upright, flinging glass and decanter off the table with a sweep of a flipper. His eyes blazed with a maniacal red fury.

'Hateful wretches! I vill drink your bloods zis night!' He lumbered forward, cloak floating in the air behind him.

SLAPPP! The first pizza hit the Count full in the face. Sonic had been expecting this any moment and his aim was perfect. As the creature mopped several kilos of pizza toppings from his face, the hedgehog leapt on to the table, jumped up to the crystal chandelier, spun crazily around on it and bounced down on to the Count's head. As he did, he saw more of the swivelling wall-mounted cameras above the shields on one wall, and he even thought he heard a faint ripple of applause.

'This is totally bogus!' he yelled to Tails as the stunned Count tried to struggle upright. 'Come on, little dude, let's find Robotnik and put a stop to all this monster nonsense!'

The furious hedgehog smashed the door down and raced into the hall. The only problem was, there were several doors leading off it and he didn't know which one might have an obese madman lurking behind it.

'Where did that bogus butler go?' Sonic asked Tails. The fox wasn't sure, but as they looked around they saw an open door far along the hall. The smell of pizza seemed to come from there as well.

'The kitchens,' Tails pointed out. 'I bet he's in there, buttling away!'

Sonic raced down the hall and straight into the kitchen. There was no sign of Ferdy among the pots, pans, and clutter of the place.

'He's hiding in the larder, the dweeb,' Sonic growled. 'Let's find him. That busybody butler may know where Robotnik is burying his bulging butt.'

The hedgehog threw open a cupboard door. He'd found the larder,. and to his delight it was absolutely packed with frozen pizza, pizza bases, packs of mozzarella cheese, and whole boxes of packs of crisps, nuts, and nachos. He just couldn't resist it, even though Tails was right behind him and yelling at him to stop. Sonic grabbed for a box full of crisps – pizza flavour, natch – but, as he did so, the floor of the larder disappeared underneath him!

Tails looked in utter horror at the empty space in front of him. One minute there had been a supercool blue hedgehog standing there, and now everything had vanished. He stared at the black abyss of space where the

larder had been. It looked like an awfully long drop and he couldn't see the bottom. As he peered really closely to figure out whether he could risk jumping after his friend, the floor of the larder came rushing up at max velocity and stopped like the top of an elevator a few centimetres below the twitching muzzle of the fox. There was no sign of Sonic.

Around him, the desperate fox heard the amplified sound of Robotnik's laughter as yet another camera swivelled around to close-up on Tails's horrified face.

'Ha ha ha! Perhaps, Spielbot, we should not make a feature film after all. With any luck, it will only be a short! Ha ha ha!'

Behind him, Tails heard the unmistakable sound of an advancing vampire. Well, he'd never heard it before, but if that half-swishing, half-chuckling noise wasn't the unmistakable sound of an advancing vampire he certainly didn't want to know what it really was. The fox whimpered softly and put his paws over his eyes.

9

NIGHTMARE ON
ROBOTNIK ST.

Sonic plummotod downwards for what seemed forever, but in fact lasted just under a second. The drop would have left most animals in a very sad – not to mention very flat – state on the stone floor he landed on, but Sonic knows how to fall and roll and he was pretty much unfazed when he picked himself up and took a look around him. As he did, the pantry-elevator he'd been thrown out of ascended behind him. Wherever he was, he was trapped.

For a moment, he thought he must be in the Chemical Plant Zone. He appeared to be in an endless, not to mention huge, subterranean chamber full of machinery. Boilers, engines and pumps hissed and battered out a rhythm of noise everywhere. He could hardly hear himself think, and thinking was hard enough to do at the best of times. Sonic wandered around, looking for a way out. He didn't find one, but at least he got away from the noisiest machines and got a little peace. He was getting angry with all this, and had just decided to do some stomping and ruin

Robotnik's machines for him when he saw Ferdy. But he wasn't a butler any longer.

He looked, well, grungy. He had a striped red and black sweater on and his face was horribly wrinkled and scarred. He had a mad grin on his face too. Most alarmingly, though, Ferdy didn't have neat little penguin flippers any more. At the end of each of his arms were a set of five very long curved blades. They looked like scalpels and they looked more than capable of shredding a hedgehog, even a superheroic megadude hedgehog, into hedgehog paté. Sonic had seen equally nasty things on Robotnik's nasty little robots before, but the way Ferdy moved around suggested he wasn't going to be as easy to get rid of as the robots Sonic knew how to deal with.

'Heh heh! Ferdy's back! Heh heh! Here's Ferdy!' the weird thing crooned as it raced for him, its blades spinning and slicing through the air. Sonic ducked its first lunge, kicked its legs from underneath it, and scampered off amongst the array of boilers and machines.

He caught Ferdy a second time with a really neat head stomp, leaping down from on top of a boiler and driving down really hard with his power sneakers. Ferdy fell over, but he got up almost immediately, his grin even wider and more horrible than before.

Oh bummer, Sonic thought grimly; this is going to be tougher than I thought! What has Robotnik been doing? I'm going to have to work really hard to stop him this time.

Sonic raced and ducked and weaved through the machinery, Ferdy in hot pursuit.

'Come to Ferdy! Ferdy's going to get you!' the ghastly thing snarled as his blades snicker-snacked ahead of it. The hedgehog was getting angrier and angrier, because he really didn't know what to do. Then he caught sight of a generator, with a large sign painted on it in big red letters: 'DANGER. EXTREMELY HIGH VOLTAGE!'. Immediately,

Sonic took hold of a power lead as thick as one of his arms and pulled really hard.

Ferdy was racing up behind him as the blue hedgehog turned almost red with the sheer effort. Sonic huffed and puffed. He strained and groaned. He pulled and wrenched, and then the lead came jerking out of the generator. The recoil was so great that Sonic lost his grip on the lead and went spinning off into the distance. The lead danced crazily, like a snake which has just eaten a raw chilli, and whipped around in the air. It struck Ferdy on his right hand, sparking off the metal.

It was a terrific firework display, the sort that really deserved a huge chorus of 'Ooohs' and Aaahs' from an appreciative crowd. A humungous number of volts generated brilliant blue sparks everywhere and Ferdy lit up a delightful blue colour, and then a rather nastier purple. It was the kind of thing which is so wonderful that adults on TV always tell you not to try this at home. When Sonic took his paws off his eyes, there wasn't much left of Ferdy apart from two sets of metal blades lying on the floor glowing cherry-red, and one smoking shoe.

Unfortunately, the other machines in the boiler room didn't seem to be anything like as pleased as Sonic. Steam was beginning to pour out of some of them and Sonic could see some pipes beginning to bulge and smoke as the lead continued to thrash around, generating great sprays of blue sparks. An alarming number of dials had needles on them hovering around the top of the red zone. That could only mean one thing: DANGER!

Sonic knew he had to get out fast. He raced around desperately looking for any sign of escape. Another few seconds could blow him into hedgehog slivers, and he knew it.

'You are doomed! Doomed! Ha ha ha!' The mocking laughter echoed around the boiler room and the frantic hedgehog's eyes nearly popped out of his head.

'Close-up on the villain!' came a smooth robotic voice.
Sonic couldn't see where it was coming from and he had no
time to look for hidden cameras. He dived underneath one
boiler just as another one, far across the room, exploded in
a huge spray of superheated steam and water.

He lay, rolled up in a ball, just hoping that the water
wouldn't flood this far across the room and boil him alive.
As he did, evil pink claws grabbed at him. Before he could
react, he was completely bound in lengths of rope which
were whipped around his spines faster than he could say
'Gimme a deep pan hot and spicy with extra cheese, hold
the olives'. The claw scrabbled around his throat and he
was dragged down into darkness. Blimey!

Spielbot was jabbering away to Robotnik. 'Wonderful,
master! Only such an awesomely wise producer could
manage to use the resources from an abandoned film to
create scenes for another one. We got wonderful angles
on the animals as they ran away! The fear on the
hedgehog's face in the boiler room was perfect! I will be
proud to be associated with this movie,' it concluded
pompously.

Eggor thought that he'd better check the specifications
for Spielbot's Grovelling Circuits; they seemed to be dangerously overactive.

'Indeed, indeed,' Robotnik gloated as he rubbed his
hands together. Unfortunately, he was so pleased that he
entirely forgot that he was holding his lunch at the time.
Egg yolk and slimy trails of egg white dripped from his
fingers on to the tiled laboratory floor. 'I selected the
chicken as the zombie template because it needed so little
change. The zombies are only slightly less intelligent than
that Chirps thing, after all. It is very important that the
template eggsperiment is as successful as my wonderful
movie,' he said to Eggor.

'Indeed, master,' Eggor said quietly. He was still programming the film crew.

'How are the preparations of the Black Tower coming along?' the madman asked Eggor, rubbing his eggy hands against his lips and slobbering a lot. That made it difficult for Eggor to hear exactly what he was saying.

'Extremely well,' Eggor said flatly. 'The last sarcophagus has just been installed.'

'Eggscellent! Make sure everything is eggspedited there.'

'We must have the right atmospherics, master,' Spielbot said. 'The lighting crew has been fitting everything to your specifications, sir.'

A special-effects robot clanked into the room. You could tell that it was a special-effects robot, not least because on its back the words 'SPECIAL EFFECTS ROBOT' were etched into the metal in gleaming futuristic letters.

'Excuse me, Assistant Director,' it said to Spielbot, 'we have a slight problem with the Phantasm Luminosity Regulator on the Grey Tower set.'

'Problem? *Problem*?' Robotnik roared. 'There are no problems! There are only solutions! I will have you melted down for scrap!' The robot scuttled away as fast as its caterpillar treads could take it.

'I shall go and deal with the problem,' Spielbot intoned smoothly. 'I will have my report within the hour, master.'

'Good robot!' Robotnik said, regaining some self-control. He smiled benignly as Spielbot headed off for the laboratory doors, which slid smoothly open before it.

'Um, master, shouldn't I be checking the Grey Tower if I'm the Director?' Eggor enquired.

'No, no, Eggor,' Robotnik said in a slightly eggsasperated tone, 'leave that to the assistant director. You should be dealing only with the really important things. Like SCUM.'

'Ah yes, the Synchronized Camera Utility Movement program,' Eggor said, slightly reassured. He'd mastered that fully.

'Spielbot is not programmed to do such important tasks. He has been fitted with Creativity Circuits and, as we all know, creative types are utterly useless at anything practical. Apart from myself, of course. That is where you eggscel, my clever Eggor. At such things as making sure than SCUM works efficiently and well. Now, is that accursed hedgehog ready for his next scene?'

Eggor almost panicked. His sensors were revealing nothing. He stalled for time. 'I have a fix on the fox, master.'

'Pah! I'm not worried about him. We can – ha ha! – eggspunge him now, for all I care. Where's Sonic?' Robotnik was quivering with pent-up rate. Speaking the hated name always made him feel like that. Little beads of sweat stood out on his pallid forehead. He looked disgusting.

'I'm afraid that Spielbot's film crew has lost track of him,' Eggor said evenly. He knew how to switch the blame when he needed to.

'What? *What??*' Robotnik wobbled with fury. It was hard to tell whether he was foaming at the mouth a little, or whether the icky stuff was just egg white dripping from his voluminous moustache. 'Quick, Eggor, we must act now! We must take the elevator to the Great Tower! If that wretched hedgehog is loose in the castle, the great eggsperiment will need completion sooner than I thought!'

Eggor felt an oily thrill run through all of his circuits as he headed with his master to the triple-locked elevator. At last, he was going to have the great eggsperiment revealed to him!

10

LAST ACTION FOR A HERO?

'Huh, so we meet again,' snarled a familiar voice. Sonic couldn't see who was talking, because a blindfold had been slapped over his face and he had been gagged as well. Being at something of a disadvantage, he tried to be polite.

'Pleased to meet you,' the hedgehog said. Well, that's what he tried to say, but it came out as something like, 'Eeneeuyeetneeu.'

'OK, Scarface, take off the sucker's gag,' the voice growled softly. 'And you can take the blindfold off, too.'

'Aw, do I have to, Boss?' whined another thin and mean voice. 'Can't I just, like, tie him up a bit tighter instead?'

'Do as I tell you or you'll be wearing concrete sneakers this time tomorrow, you dirty little rat,' the first voice snarled again.

Before the blindfold was reluctantly removed by the grubby rodent minion, Sonic had realized who had captured him: Capone and his rats! He'd met them before and they were mean dudes. He groaned and his tummy

gave a little lurch in sympathy. He'd have been better off being chased by Robotnik's robots than being in the clutches of the rat gang.

Capone had changed a little since he'd last seen him. He was still a very big, sleek, scarred black rat, but in addition to his shades (which even Sonic had to admit were fairly cool) he was wearing a particularly neat line in pinstripe suits these days. Yeah, it was too traditional by superdude hedgehog standards, but it seemed to suit him. The massive rat bit the end off a cigar and stuck it in his mouth. A female rat moll leaned across and lit it for him. The rat breathed in the smoke and coughed rather horribly. Looking faintly disgusted, it threw the cigar to the ground.

'One of Robotnik's cheap imitations!' he snarled. 'That makes me feel mean. You like-a that I feel mean, hedgehog?'

'You're looking way cool in those bodacious threads,' Sonic said. Flattery, he hoped, would get him somewhere.

'Flattery will get you nowhere,' snarled the huge rat. 'And don't forget to call me Your Majesty, 'cos I'm King Rat, remember? If you don't remember, Scarface here will stimulate your memory with his gold tie pin. Now, look, sucker, let's get to the point. You're in this big movie Robotnik's making, right?'

'Um, right, Your Maj.' Sonic played for time. He had to find out what Capone wanted, fool him into thinking he could get it for him, then run away.

'Don't play for time, sucker. Don't think you can find out what I want, fool me into thinking you can get it for me, then run away,' the rat growled.

'It had never crossed my mind, Bodacious Majesty Dude,' Sonic said politely, but inside he was beginning to wonder: *how did he do that?*

'Well, look, sucker. You got a good part in this movie, right?' The large rat loomed over Sonic. The twenty or so rats standing behind him moved a bit closer too. One or two of them were licking their lips, and Sonic was sure one was talking to his companion out of the side of his mouth about spine removal and hedgehog pizza.

'Yup,' Sonic said, trying to sound brave. 'I've been in all the big scenes so far, your Maj!'

'Huh,' Capone sniffed, but Sonic could see that the rat believed him. He guessed that the rat wanted a piece of the action.

'Okay, I believe you. I want a piece of the action, right?'

'How do you do that?' Sonic asked him, puzzled.

'Do what?'

'Keep reading the script one line late?' Capone gave him a puzzled look in return. 'Oh well, it doesn't matter, super-dude,' said Sonic. 'I guess it just shows you must have a radically natural acting talent,' the hedgehog said, trying to charm his way out of his situation.

'Huh. Well see here, you spiny blue freak, my little Chloe here says I'd kinda look good in a movie, you got me?' The female rat on Capone's arm simpered and waved her feathered neck scarf at the hedgehog. 'Now you tell me what kinda movie this is, and how you gonna get me a lead role, right?'

'Don't forget the Big Guns, Your Majesty,' piped up a small voice at the back of the rat pack.

'Shuddupayaface!' Capone bellowed. 'I do the talking when we're dealing with freaks, right?' Sonic was getting angry now. Being called a freak twice inside a minute was too much for him.

'You asked me to remind you, Your Majesty,' the unseen rat said defensively. 'Just after we dumped Dillinger in the Mega Mack back in the Chemical Plant Zone.'

'Oh yeah, right,' Capone growled softly. 'Well, look, it's gonna be a heroic action movie, right? With lotsa Big Guns and shoot-outs and heists and that kinda stuff, you got me?'

The beginnings of a Really Brilliant Idea began to form in Sonic's brain. Actually, it was an Incredibly Stupid Idea except for one huge advantage: it was born of total ignorance of what Eggor was doing, and that made it a Really Brilliant Idea.

'You know, it's funny you should say that,' Sonic began . . .

Tails peeped through his paws. Above him towered the Count. His appearance had changed, and not for the better. Now he was wearing a top hat and a quite exceptionally silly pair of round-lensed, purple-tinted glasses perched on his nose.

'Eeeek! Don't bite me!' Tails pleaded.

'Vhy vould I vant to bite you?' the Count said in a slightly hurt tone of voice.

'Because you're a vampire and you want to drink my blood! And then I'll be a vampire and it'll be really 'orrible! I won't be able to play in the sunshine in the Green Hill Zone in the mornings! All my friends will tease me and call me names because I'll be so pale and weedy!' The fox was close to tears. His best friend was lost, and he felt very alone.

'Oh, look, just because I am killing people and drinking zeir blood doesn't make me a bad person,' the Count said gently. 'I'm qvite sensitive, you know.'

'Sensitive?' Tails was staggered.

'Oh yah. I am reading poetry,' the County said, looking a tad defensive. Then he brightened up and pulled a small, leather-bound book from his jacket pocket. 'Vould you like me to read you some?'

'Not just now, thank you all the same,' Tails said, regaining some composure. At last, the fact that he had some chance of escape from this deranged vampire-walrus had occurred to him, and he just wanted to get away. But the walrus was very large and there was no way of racing past him. 'But, um, I notice you look rather different now. Not so, well, aggressive.' What he wanted to say was not so barking mad, despite the ridiculous glasses, but that seemed rather impolite and Tails was a well-brought-up-fox.

'Ah, appearances are zo superficial. Master Tails, ve vampires haff very complicated personalities,' the Count replied.

'You do?'

'Indeed. Sometimes ve are ravening beasts, desperate for ze taste of blood!' The Count's eyes flashed red and he seemed to grow a metre in height as he stood over the cowering fox, flippers outstretched, his cloak covering the entire length of the passage.

'Eek! Yikes!'

'But zat is being only part of ze time,' the Count said as he settled back down to his smaller size. Now he looked almost kindly. 'At ozer times, ve lament our sad fate, and zen ve are getting very miserable.'

'You are?'

'Yah. And sensitive.'

'Zat too? Er, I mean, that too?'

'Look, I've told you zat I read poetry, haven't I? Sometimes I even write it myself, in my diaries.

'Oh, bogus! No, I mean, that's really deep. I wish I could write poetry.' Tails shouldn't have told lies. He knew it always got him into trouble.

'Vell, perhaps you could. I shall read you some of my poetry and zen you may learn somezing.'

Tails realized that he had really got himself into deep, deep trouble this time, but there was no escaping his awful fate. Wearily, he trudged back to the feast hall, with only the prospect of an hour of listening to bad vampire poetry stretching out ahead of him. What a bummer!

*   *   *

If Eggor had had a flabber, it would have been gasted. He had simply had no idea how grand the master's scheme was. Now that he'd seen the monster for the final scene, he was more determined than ever to make sure he looked terrific in it. But he still wanted to do some directing, and he needed to find that wretched hedgehog. Frantically, he flicked between his battery of sensor inputs from the banks of computers in the lab centre, Finally, he found the input he was looking for. The indicator blinked a pleasing red on the scanners. There were some other things with the hedgehog, but Eggor wasn't too worried about them.

Yes! So close to my film crew, too, Eggor thought. This is a perfect chance to shoot that spare footage.

He began to type in a string of commands at his keyboard and sat back to admire his work, a thin robot grin playing on his metal face. Master will be so pleased . . .

11

THE RAT PACK MOVIE

'I said I want a good action movie. What's this bogus nonsense about a multi-genre cinematic experience, you snivelling little weirdo?' Capone growled. He didn't understand what Sonic was saying, and that made him feel anxious. He was worried that some other rat might be smarter than he was and be able to figure out what Sonic was saying. That would make him look dumb. Capone liked looking dumb about as much as he liked someone treading on his sleek pink tail. In other words, Not At All.

'It's a term that we hip jive film-types use,' Sonic said airily. He hated speaking like that, but he thought that was how film and television people sounded so he tried to imitate them as best he could. It meant disconnecting his brain and talking gibberish, but he felt like he could get used to it. Maybe.

'You mean, like journalists?' Capone sneered.

'Yeah, I suppose so,' Sonic said certainly.

'We had a visit from a journalist once,' Capone said quietly. Sonic didn't realise what he was letting himself in for.

'Oh really? I guess that was kinda fab-groovy, although not as good as the hip-dude movie guys we're going to share space with,' he managed to say. He really did hate talking like that.

'Yeah,' Capone drawled slowly. 'He was gonna write somethin' about us, wasn't he, guys? Somethin' about rodents from disadvantaged backgrounds?'

There were growls and sniggers from the rat pack. 'Yeah. Affirmative action for rats or somefink,' one rat growled. 'But he didn't bring us any pizza, though.' That had clearly rankled the rats a lot. They all growled at the memory.

'Well,' Capone snarled as he grabbed Sonic by the throat, 'he was a pretentious little dweeb who talked like he'd swallowed a dictionary –'

'Er, yes, well, the film people we'll meet, they're not like that at all, Your Maj. Oh no,' Sonic groaned. If only the rats would untie him! With his paws tied tightly behind his back, and his legs bound so that he could only take tiny steps forward, there wasn't much he could do to escape.

'Well, that's good,' Capone jeered. 'Like I say, we want an action movie, right? Like that scene you had in the boiler room. Lotsa explosions and things going bang, right?'

The rat pack cheered.

'And I get to look especially cool with Chloe here, right?'

The rat pack cheered again, but a bit less convincingly this time.

'With REAL BIG GUNS, right?'

The rat pack cheered like someone had just given them their own weight in deep-pan pizzas.

'Weeeellll,' Sonic said, 'there are no big guns as such, Majestic dude. But there's something better than that.'

'You mean military weapons? Hey guys, we're gonna drive tanks! Woweee!' Capone gloated.

'Er, not quite. But almost as good,' Sonic said hurriedly.

Drawing himself up to his full height, he pronounced as loftily as he could, 'The Ebon Staff of Peaminster the Magnificent!'

Capone grabbed him by the throat again. Sonic was getting very tired of this by now. Capone's breath smelt like he'd never cleaned his teeth, *ever*, which was actually exactly how often he had cleaned them. His tongue was furry with that kind of fur that grows on face flannels left for months in a corner of a grungy bathroom. It rated a set of straight tens on the grossometer.

'What is this Peaminster garbage? You make me look dumb in front of my boys and you're one ex-hedgehog,' the rat hissed into Sonic's ear. Just to make the point clear, he snapped his grody yellow-green teeth about a millimetre from Sonic's left ear. Wincing a little the hedgehog played his trump card.

'It's the best flamethrower on Mobius, Maj,' he said.

Capone's beady eyes gleamed with pleasure. 'Well, why didn't ya say so? Youse guys, you hear that? Flamethrowers!'

The rat pack cheered wildly.

The assistant to the assistant director was confused. Hurriedly, he began issuing orders to the camera-toting robots around it. They were modified Cluckers, without guns, but with swivelling cameras mounted around their turrets. Except for the First Camerabot, that is; that was a whizzing Nebula with camera lenses everywhere, used for special angle shots. With its zoom lenses shooting in and out of focus everywhere it looked very peculiar indeed.

'Um, luvvies,' the assistant said hopefully, clapping its hands together. The humans turned to look at the robot expectantly, breaking off their mutterings about piece rates and gala openings and first nights. Sir Norbert stopped bobbing his hair.

'Big scene coming up, luvs! Apparently the producer has changed his mind again,' the robot said.

'Oh, these media moguls, they're so fickle,' moaned Drizzle, wringing his hands. 'And I haven't even been to Make-up yet.'

'It's the big fight scene against the wererats!' the robot exclaimed.

'Wererats?' Thug said blankly. That word wasn't in his vocabulary. Actually, pretty much any old word wasn't in his vocabulary, but he at least knew how to repeat a word when he heard one even if he couldn't remember it.

'Yeah,' the assistant said, scanning the print out which had just arrived from the Central Studio. 'Dozens of 'em. They're holding a hedgehog prisoner. You have to defeat them while making sure the hedgehog doesn't get wasted.'

'Do I get to use the Ebon Staff of –' Drizzle began.

'As much as you want, but keep it away from the hedgehog,' the robot interrupted him.

'Oh, and I think the petrol's running low,' Drizzle muttered. 'Can I get a top-up?'

'No time, luvvie!' the robot yelled. 'We're going for a take! Cameras! Lights! Action!'

The rats stormed into the passageway ahead. With a great snarling war cry, they hurtled towards the humans. Some carried long, heavy pins in their trembling paws. Most of them had ropes for tying up people. Two of them had violin cases, but violins aren't terrifically useful weapons when it comes right down to the real nitty-gritty. One of them had a tactical nuclear weapon, or least he thought he did, because he suffered from delusions of grandeur and didn't realize that it was actually a wooden lollipop stick. His attempt to launch it wasn't terribly successful.

Drizzle pointed his staff down the passageway, intending to turn the rats into small smoking lumps of

73

carbon. Unfortunately, when he pressed the concealed button a couple of drops of petrol dripped from the end of it and nothing happened. The furious actor turned the staff around to inspect the far end of it and a tiny puff of flame shot out, setting his hair on fire.

The mayhem didn't last too long. The actress smothered Drizzle's head in a blanket before he could come to any serious harm, and Sir Norbert was swiftly overwhelmed by gleeful rats who had him tied up within seconds. Capone took one look at Thug and played a master stroke.

'Okay, dude, what's the square foot of seven then?' It was something Capone had never figured out at rat school, and he sure knew a kindred spirit when he saw one. Thug's brain cell grappled with the problem for some time and then gave up the effort. The huge brute's face contorted with mental strain, his eyes rolled back in his head and he fell unconscious to the floor.

Capone pounced on Thug's chest and yelled to the cowering Chloe to come over. Standing proudly, arms akimbo, he demanded attention.

'Hey, you!' he yelled to the directing robot. 'Get those cameras on me, you get me? Chloe, just kinda fall at my heroic feet and look adoring, babe.'

'Help! Help! I have been bitten by an horrendous wererat!' Sir Norbert moaned. 'Foul lycanthropy! I shall have to seek atonement and a healer forthwith, ere I be transformed!'

'What's that chinless dweeb wailing on about?' Capone snarled, 'Hey, you, metal man! Put a sock in it. The noise is spoiling my big speech.'

Sonic looked at the madhouse of struggling humans, preening rats and the film crew, and decided it was time to get the heck out of here. He'd managed to slip the knot tying his paws behind his back in all the confusion, and he shuffled off into a dark corner to free himself. In a few

seconds, he was able to turn tail and speed off along the passages below Castle Robotnik, looking for another way back inside.

'Now, isn't zat just a vonderful use of metaphor?' the Count beamed at Tails.

The fox was having a hard time of it. Poetry bored him rigid and the vampire seemed to be able to drone on about it for hours and hours.

'Oh, erm, yeah, like, awesome,' Tails groaned. Feigning enthusiasm was beyond him by now. He was stiff from sitting in his armchair, so he got up to stretch his legs (and tails). His bleary eyes told him that it was getting awfully late. Walking to the window of the lounge, he pulled open the curtains.

The terrible storm outside had abated. Watery sunshine streamed into the room. It was just after dawn. The Count shrieked and put his flippers over his eyes.

'Ach! Sunshine! Deadly!' he cried in alarm.

'I like sunshine. It's warm and nice and healthy,' the fox replied, somewhat cheered up by the view outside.

'No it isn't,' the vampire snarled. 'Sunshine is giving people horrible diseases. Malignant melanoma for a start, and zat's just for normal people.'

'Erm, er,' Tails stuttered. He hadn't a clue what old Fang Features was dribbling on about.

'And it's lethal to vampires!' the Count hissed, backing away to the door. 'Close zose curtains at vonce!'

Tails realised at once that he could extricate himself from the Count's clutches. He needed a well-argued reason not to close the curtains, because he didn't want to really anger the Count. He might meet him again, after all.

The trouble is, 'Shan't!' was the best he could come up with in the time allowed. The Count glared at him with hate-filled bloodshot eyes and fled down the corridor to his daytime resting place, screaming that the fox hadn't seen ze last of him yet. Tails was free of him, but he was also alone again and he didn't know where Sonic was. His hedgehoggy pal had been gone an awfully long time.

Tails knew that he ought to go to the kitchens to find out if he could use the same elevator that had taken Sonic into the castle dungeons, but he was also curious. The Count had brought a whole heap of poetry books from what was plainly a library situated next door to the lounge, so the fox sneaked in to take a look around.

Tails sniffed underneath the large desks in the room, and checked out the fireplace, but there wasn't anything unusual. Getting up again, he heard the tall tale whir of a camera swivelling above his head. Leaping backwards, he hit a bookcase next to a wall, and as he did it pivoted around to reveal a secret castle passage behind it. Before he could react, the fox was plunged into darkness and the bookcase swivelled firmly closed behind him, and he couldn't budge it. Robotnik's mad laughter echoed all around.

'Spielbot, activate the camera units in the Black Tower,' Robotnik snarled. 'We are about to dispose of an unnecessary film eggstra!'

Tails whimpered and padded forwards into the unknown blackness.

12

INTO THE BLACK TOWER!

Sonic was in unfamiliar territory. The dismal, smelly passages below the castle really did seem to go on for ever. He didn't know where he was, and he had no way of getting his bearings. Comforting himself with some soggy crisps he found in the corner of one of his pockets, he plodded along, hoping Tails was safe somewhere. At least Robotnik didn't seem to have any cameras filming him as he walked along – or at least he couldn't see any. Then he heard the padding of paws heading toward him.

'Hey, dude, is this the set for the Castle Robotnik movie?' came a familiar-sounding voice.

'Johnny?' the hedgehog said uncertainly. It really did sound just like Johnny Lightfoot.

'Er, no. Call me Jase,' the rabbit said as it turned the corner ahead of Sonic and loomed into view. Sonic didn't like the look of him at all. He was wearing something which looked like the kind of face-mask ice hockey players wear to stop their teeth being smashed in and he had something in a large leather bag he was carrying.

'I have a really good part in the movie,' the rabbit said rather unpleasantly. Sonic realized that if Tails's theory about the castle and its denizens was correct, this thing was going to turn out to be some kind of monster. Having narrowly escaped some impromptu spine-trimming at the hands of the penguin butler, he just wanted to get away. But the rabbit blocked the way ahead and Sonic certainly didn't want to go back to the madness of the film crew and the rats behind him.

'Well, that's truly bodacious,' the hedgehog lied, somewhat alarmed by the manner in which the rabbit was pulling at something large inside his bag. He decided to try to confuse him. 'But, like, do you have a good agent, man?'

The rabbit looked pleasingly confused for a moment and stopped what he was doing. 'What do you mean?' he enquired.

'Well, let's put it this way. This Robotnik dude, he doesn't pay the kind of fees top actors should get. A really good agent could make sure you get oodles of megabucks!' He hoped this would confuse the rabbit long enough for him to talk his way past it. It didn't work.

'I'm not getting paid,' the rabbit snarled, pulling at whatever was inside his bag again. Sonic thought he heard a whirring noise, which then stalled.

'That's outrageous! Let me, like, act as your agent and I can make sure you get paid serious carrots,' the hedgehog said hurriedly.

'I'm not doing it for the money. Or the carrots. I don't eat carrots anyway.'

'Really?'

'Yeah. I'm doing it for the artistic integrity and the creative product values,' the rabbit lied. 'But most of all, I'm doing it because I'm a total homicidal maniac – and because of *this*!'

The whirring thing inside the bag, pulled into life by the

rabbit's paws, shredded it to pieces. Holding the chainsaw aloft, the mad-eyed rabbit lunged at Sonic. Or rather, where Sonic had just been.

Sonic wasn't going to stay and fight Jase. He knew he could defeat the rabbit, but the really awful thought was that those whirling saw-teeth might just shear his spines off and that would be too heinous to even think about. Leaping over the chainsaw as the rabbit brought it down towards him, he shot off into the unknown.

Before long, the torches had disappeared from the walls and there was no light. Sonic was running in pitch darkness. The whir of the chainsaw buzzed angrily, getting louder and louder behind him. He couldn't see anything of where he was going, which really explains why he suddenly ran full pelt into something soft which crumpled when he hit it. The hedgehog went flying head over heels, and the relentless whir-whir-whir got horribly, inevitably, closer.

'Yikes, my head!' snivelled whatever it was that Sonic had collided with. By a stroke of genius, Sonic realised he'd bumped into Tails.

'Tails! Buddy! Are you all right, little dude?' The hedgehog asked nervously. Jase and his chainsaw were getting *very* close now. 'Look, I'd like to say I'm most radically sorry but unless you want to be fox steaks, we have to keep running. There's a deranged rabbit with a chainsaw after me!'

Tails could hear the noise and he needed no second invitation to zip along on the heels of the fleeing hedgehog. By some miracle, they managed not to fall over in the darkness, and everything seemed to be going all right until Sonic ran straight into a door and almost knocked himself out. The chainsaw, once getting fainter behind them, began to get louder again.

'Why doesn't he fall over and turn himself into bunny

chunks?' Sonic groaned, sure he was seeing little gold rings spinning around his head. Feeling around with his paws, he realised he was in a dead end. With a homicidal, chainsaw-armed bunny rabbit closing in for the kill, things did not look good.

Jase was virtually on top of them when Sonic crouched low, leapt over him, and gave him a spin kick. The rabbit flew forwards and his chainsaw screamed in protest as it hit the door. The whirling metal teeth of the saw carved a huge hole in it, and the rabbit fell through. There was a long, long scream and the sound of a demented killer rabbit hitting something very hard a long, long way down, and finally a rather nasty sound from the chainsaw which suggested that that particular bunny had scoffed his last carrot.

Sonic peered through the hole in the doorway. A faint, pale light came from inside, but a cloud of dust was still settling. A very deep pit lay just inside the door, but further across he could see a set of stone steps leading to another door. He knew that he and Tails could easily make it across. They had to. There wasn't anywhere else to go.

'They're in the Black Tower then,' Eggor said in a matter-of-fact voice.

Spielbot had his visual sensors stuffed into a very large book, and didn't say anything. Eggor was itching to know what was in the book, but he didn't want Spielbot to think he was that keenly interested. In the end, his curiosity got the better of him.

'What's that then?' he said laconically.

'What's what?' Spielbot said innocently.

'That book,' Eggor replied testily. 'What is in it? Why is it so fascinating?'

'Well, it gave me the idea for part of the Master's design for the Grey Tower. The monster in the basement.'

'Oh, yes, that,' Eggor said dismissively. Actually, he couldn't remember what the monster was offhand.

'It's an old script for a movie which unfortunately didn't get finished. One of mine actually,' Spielbot continued. 'It was a film about huge prehistoric killer pigs on the loose in a theme park. Unfortunately, we couldn't get enough wood to build the actors.'

'Oh really?' Eggor said dubiously. Then he caught sight of the title of the book: *Jurassic Pork*.

At that moment, Robotnik wobbled into the laboratory. He was in a bad mood this morning. He had a slight head cold and that always made him very short-tempered. Having lost his sense of taste, he'd put too much tabasco in his raw egg breakfast and now his tongue was burning too.

'Well, Eggor? How is it going? It had better be going eggscellently well,' the madman snarled. 'I feel like melting some robots down for scrap today.'

'They are just entering the Black Tower,' Eggor said hurriedly. 'They've crossed the pit, and now they're trying to figure out how to get through the next door.'

'Well, then, open it by remote control! Let us – ha ha! – let us see how they deal with the traps in there,' Robotnik gloated. He was feeling better already.

Tails and Sonic couldn't figure out the weird chamber they'd got into at all. All over the walls, and on the door before them, were very odd and stylised paintings and symbols. They showed various heavily suntanned animals standing around giant stone pyramids, apparently dancing in very weird zigzag postures. All the females seemed to be dressed in very little but wearing their own weight in mascara, if the shadows around their eyes were anything to go by. It all looked very strange.

'Oh look! There's a little doorbell here,' Tails said brightly. 'There something written beside it as well. I can't quite . . . . Oh yes: *Toot 'n' come in*. Isn't that friendly?' His tails wagged ever so slightly. He was easily pleased sometimes.

'Don't be ridiculous,' Sonic snapped. 'This is some-where below Castle Robotnik. You think we're going to get a gala welcome?' Then he was sorry, for Tails's tails drooped and he looked very miserable all of a sudden, and anything which lightened their spirits would have been welcome, no matter how silly. They were tired now, having been kept awake all night by homicidal maniacs and poetry readers.

'Anyway, I'm not ringing any doorbell,' Sonic growled. 'You never know when some sort of massive electrical shock is going to zap right up one's spines.' So saying, he took a flying spinning leap at the door and smashed it down.

The room beyond was completely bare, except for a pair of very odd-looking metal statues. They had the heads of jackals, not one of Sonic's favourite animals, and the bodies of crocodiles, another of Sonic's unfavourite animals, but they were standing upright. Sonic didn't like the look of them at all. But, if he and Tails were going to get to the door opposite them, they were going to have to walk right between them.

'What are they?' Tails whispered.

'Search me, dude. Jackodiles, I guess,' Sonic said tartly.

'I've never heard of those,' Tails replied, sounding highly dubious.

'Well, then, maybe they're crockals. I don't know. Who cares? More of Robotnik's creations. I think we should . . .' He turned to whisper in Tails's ears just as Eggor flipped the activation switch and the statues lumbered into life.

Fortunately, it was exactly what Sonic had been expecting all along, and he and Tails were raring to go.

They leapt into the fray, stomping the robots with ease. Sonic's SuperSpin was more than enough for one of them, which fell apart very pleasingly, and Tails ducked, dodged and finally stomped the other.

'Ha! Child's play! You hear that, you eggy lunatic?' Sonic yelled, hoping Robotnik could hear what he was saying. Unfortunately, Eggor had programmed a malfunction into the sound relay circuits. He didn't want Robotnik to go berserk and have him melted down for scrap, and as a result Robotnik never heard a word.

Sonic charged for the next door, smashing it into flying strips of wood. Racing down the stone steps beyond, followed by Tails, he ran straight into Robotnik's next dastardly trap. Above him, he heard a swishing sound and he looked up just in time to see doors swing open in the ceiling and a huge stone ball drop into the stairway. It made a deafening noise as it crunched into the stone steps, and then began to roll towards them, slowly at first but definitely gathering speed.

'Yikes! We're going to be squashed!' Tails yelped. As the stone ball got closer, they could see just how huge it was. It virtually filled the stairway, so there was no chance of jumping over it. There weren't any side-passages along the stairs either. There was only one thing to do: the friends took to their heels and ran like crazy!

'Uh-oh, look out! Time for a pit stop!' yelled Sonic as they came to a screeching halt before another great hole in the ground. It was far too wide even for them to jump across, and they couldn't even see the bottom of it. Safety was an unbridgeable gap away on the other side. Robotnik's gloating laughter mocked them from unseen loudspeakers.

'Now – ha ha ha! – now we will play my favourite game!' he sneered. 'Not football or racing or soccer. *Squash!*

'We're doomed! Doomed, I tell you!' Tails panicked as the ball rumbled ever closer.

'Not yet,' Sonic growled. He whipped out a length of rope he had secreted about his person. 'Those rats tied me up awfully well; I didn't expect to have to thank them for it.' He made a noose out of the end of the rope and whirled it across the chasm. It caught something, and when he tugged at it, it held safely.

'Get across, buddy,' the hedgehog ordered. 'I'll hold one end and you can get over.'

'But what about you? How will you make it?' Tails asked anxiously.

'Dude, this is no time to worry over details. When you get across, just hold your end really tight,' Sonic gasped. There was no time to waste. Tails gripped the rope in all four paws and scrabbled across the pit to the safety of the other side.

He saw Sonic take the other end of the rope and launch himself just as the stone ball rolled over and down. Oddly enough, there wasn't the tremendous crash Tails was expecting as the ball hit the bottom of the pit, which he thought must mean that it probably went all the way through the other side of Mobius. He had a sudden image of a little fox, just like him but wearing a hat decorated with corks and holding a bent stick, peering down a huge hole just like this one, only to be very surprised by a blooming great oversized marble which shot up out of the ground at him.

Shaking such a stupid idea out of his head, Tails anchored the rope safely to the door handle around which Sonic had managed to loop the noose when he threw it. Slowly, he advanced to the edge of the pit to see what had become of his friend. When he got to the very edge, he could see the rope had frayed into a few very thin strands against the ragged rock. If he tugged on it to try to bring

Sonic up, the rope would snap. Peering down, he could only see dust and darkness.

'Sonic? Sonic? Where are you?' he called out timidly, a rising edge of panic in his voice.

He didn't get a reply.

13

I WANT MY MUMMY!

Sonic found himself dangling precariously on the rope. Holding on tightly with his paws, he could feel that there must be something wrong. It felt too frail, and he didn't dare try to swing on it. If he could have done that, he would have been able to swing against the side of the pit and get some momentum going for an upwards spin, but as it was he was just hanging. He looked down and saw a pit full of hissing snakes only a few metres below him. He gulped.

'Greetingsss, Missster Jonesss,' hissed a green snake with yellow eyes and a very oddly-shaped head.

'Mister Jones?' the hedgehog repeated, somewhat taken aback.

'Oh, all right then,' the snake said rather irritably, '*Doctor* Jonesss, if you mussst. We don't usually ssstand on sscer-emony in these action ssscenesss, you know.'

'Jones? Who were you expecting? My name's Sonic, you silly serpent,' Sonic muttered. This was just too much. This wretched reptile didn't even recognise a world-

famous hedgehog when he saw one, and there was only one to see, after all.

'You're not Doctor Jonesss?' the snake said suspiciously, rearing up and swaying from side to side. Its forked tongue flicked in and out of its narrow tongue, and its beady gaze never left Sonic for an instant.

'No I'm not. I'm a hedgehog, for heaven's sake,' Sonic snapped in an exasperated voice.

'Hmmmm. Ssso you are. Well, I sssuppossse you are if you sssay you are,' the snake said disappointedly. 'Never ssseen one before, you sssee. The name's Basil, by the way.'

'Sonic the world-famous hedgehog and all-round good guy superhero; pleased to meet you, I'm sure. Now, um . . .' Sonic was about to ask how he could get out when something occurred to him. 'Where did that stone ball go?'

'Oh, that,' the snake replied rather airily with a loud snakey sniff, 'I expect Ssspecial Effectsss dealt with that. Happensss all the time, you know.'

'Oh, really? Well, um, is there any way out of that pit? I've fallen and I can't get up,' Sonic grumbled.

'No, there'sss no way out apart from the sssecret door behind the huge ssstatue of Pharaoh Goateses over there in that corner,' the snake indicated with a flick of his head. 'So you're trapped, matey.'

'But there's a secret door. So there is a way out,' Sonic contradicted confidently. The snake looked startled by that.

'Yes, but you don't know that,' he snapped. 'It's a secret door, right?'

'Oh yes I do. You just told me.'

The snake sighed. His silly hissing accent appeared to vanish. 'This isn't going to be easy, is it, Jones – um, I mean, Sonic. Ha! Oh, wait, I know. I'll hypnotise you!' He swayed his head from side to side and stared at the hedgehog dangling on the rope. Sonic thought he was crazy and said so.

'It doesn't work? Are you sure?' the snake said incredulously.

'No,' Sonic said flatly.

'Hmmmm. My swaying hypnotic dance is definitely supposed to work,' the snake said, clearly miffed by this turn of events. 'I learned it from the mongoose that offed my dear old granny. I *am* going to hypnotise you, blast it,' the snake said finally and took a pocket watch from the floor. Holding it in his jaws, he swung it to and fro.

'Look at the watch and listen to my voice. Your eyes are getting heavy ... Your eyes are getting very, very heavy . . .' His voice sounded very strange through his clenched jaws.

'Of course they are,' Sonic explained cheerily. 'But what do you expect? I haven't slept all night. I've been chased by deranged animals with chainsaws!'

'You are feeling sleepy!'

'I just told you that!'

The snake dropped the watch. 'Oh, I give up,' he exclaimed. 'Go on then, you rotten spoilsport. Third statue on the right. Watch out, because it'll make an awful mess when you smash it down.'

'What about all those snakes, though? I mean, are they poisonous?' Sonic asked fretfully.

'Nah, they're not even real snakes,' Basil sniffed. 'Just wriggling rubbery tubes. They're really tacky.'

The faint call of a worried fox could be heard far in the distance, interrupting their conversation.

'It's okay, dude. Float on down!' Sonic yelled. 'I wouldn't, like, object too much if you picked me up on the way.'

The twin-tail-powered fox spiralled slowly down into the pit. Seeing the writhing snakes, he hovered worriedly above Sonic.

'Yikes! Are you sure about this?' he fretted.

'Radically safe, dude. They're all made of rubber,' Sonic sniffed. 'Just look at 'em. Bogus or what?'

'Hello. Have you ever been hypnotised?' Basil enquired of Tails, getting his watch out hopefully.

'Don't try that with me,' Tails said airily. 'My grandpa was trained by the Hyponotising Mongeese of the Emerald Hill Zone!' Basil shrank back hastily while Tails shot Sonic a crafty wink.

Right then the rope holding Sonic snapped, but Tails just managed to grab him as he plummeted downwards. Rather awkwardly, they managed to spiral down into a heap among the wriggling rubber snakes.

'Yuk, gross,' Tails sniffed. 'I hate rubber snakes. And those 'orrible spiders made out of felt.'

'Yeah, know what you mean,' Sonic said absent-mindedly. He was busy sizing up the statue of Goateses the Pharaoh, figuring out the best place to take a flying leap at it.

'And Johnny's luminous rubber chicken too.'

'Yeah, that too,' Sonic sniffed. He wasn't listening at all now. He'd seen the join between the head and body of the statue.

'And, you know, what I really hate is that 'orrid green slimy slime stuff they sell in pots. Someone put a cupful in my bed once. I didn't see it because I was so tired, and it got all in my fur. It was disgusting,' Tails said loudly with the air of someone who is very suspicious of the person he's talking to. Sonic turned rather angrily to his friend.

'Chill out, dude! That's not important right now. Look,' and he pointed to the statue. 'He says there's a secret door behind the statue,' looking at Basil.

'Yeah, that's right, mate,' the snake said, swaying a little in the hope of hypnotising Tails just a little bit. He looked even more disappointed than ever when Tails gave him a look which plainly indicated that the fox thought he was one topping short of a full pizza.

'What's behind that, then?' Tails asked. Sonic looked a little sheepish, realising that that simple question had never occurred to him.

'The burial chamber of the High Priestess of the Pharaoh Goateses,' the snake said pompously.

'Look, you over-animated dipstick,' Sonic said angrily, 'this isn't a real pyramid. It's all bogus. This is Castle Robotnik. Now, what's really in there?'

'Well, I don't know,' the snake replied, rather irked. 'That's what it said it was in the script. I mean, I've never been in there, have I? It's secret, how many times do I have to tell you? Cripes, there's no pleasing some people.'

'Well, there's nothing else for it then, I suppose we'll have to go in there,' Tails decided and turned to look at Sonic.

There was an empty space where the hedgehog had been standing, and a tremendous bang as the statue of the Pharaoh crashed to the floor. As the dust settled, Tails could see a very narrow duct set into the wall behind where the head of the statue had been. Sonic was already scrabbling along it. Tails clambered perilously up on the pile of statue rubble to follow him. It was very dark, very dusty and very smelly, and he didn't care for it at all.

'Phew! I'm exhausted,' Tails groaned, wiping perspiration from his brow with his paws. A thin film of grime from the dust was all over him. 'I haven't slept all night, and my eyes hurt.'

'Yeah,' Sonic groaned. Even after stuffing his face with most of the nuts and crisps Tails had left, fatigue was catching up with him too. He'd put in enough superfast running and SuperSpins for one day and night, what with Ferdy and Jase and all the rats, and his limbs felt very

heavy indeed. Why, perhaps that crafty snake had hypnotised him after all!

'Look, a door. We're at the end of this endless passage
at last,' Tails said with new heart. 'And hey! There's an
inscription on it.'

It was difficult to read the letters on the plaque, because
there was virtually no light left at all. It was also difficult
because the letters were written in weird hieroglyphs and,
as such, were completely incomprehensible anyway.

'I wonder if the Roaming Romans wrote this?' Tails
pondered. 'Did they build pyramids and stuff?'

'Dunno. History never was my strong point,' Sonic con-
fessed. 'I tend to be better at – smashing down doors!'

A few seconds later, he had proved his point.

What they found on the other side of the door amazed
them.

'Wow. This is mind-boggling. I mean, I know it's bogus
'cos it's all been made by Robotnik and everything, but it's
still awesome!' Tails said shakily.

The burial chamber seemed to be totally filled with gold,
like, everywhere. Fabulous statues of jackal-headed
beasts and serving attendants to the High Priestess stood
twice the size of either Sonic or Tails. Huge gold urns and
vases stood in serried ranks alongside a set of gold-inlaid
marble steps leading up to the sarcophagus of the Priestess herself. It stood upright, with the image of the Priestess engraved in vivid cobalt blue, black, white and gold on
its face.

'Hmmm. This could be a Roman urn,' Sonic said, idly
checking out the first thing he saw.

'What's a Roman urn?' Tails asked.

'About two-fifty a week, I think,' Sonic sniggered, hardly
able to believe his luck. Guess that was one of the func-
tions of keeping a sidekick around: they always knew when
to feed you a gag line. 'Hmm. I don't know about this. Does

that ancient female-type princess dude look vaguely familiar to you?'

There was the faintest suggestion of a creak from somewhere in the room. They didn't notice it.

Nervously, Tails walked to the foot of the steps and looked at the sarcophagus a little more closely.

'Now you come to mention it, there is something familiar about it. Can't quite place it, though,' he puzzled.

The creak suggested itself more loudly. Sonic looked back down the duct, thinking that the rubble must still be settling from the shattered statue of the Pharaoh.

'Me neither,' the hedgehog sighed as he fastened his gaze on the tomb once again.

The creak decided to ignore suggestion and go for something a bit more blatant.

'Did you hear something?' Tails said fretfully. Although everything was so rich in this strange place, his nerves were a bit frayed from sleeplessness.

'I think it's that rubble back in the snake pit,' Sonic said uneasily. 'It's still settling, I suppose.'

The creak gave up on blatant and went for overkill. It sounded like your granny's false teeth being prised apart by a champion wrestler and the resultant sound being whacked through a 6000-watt amplifier.

Tails almost jumped into Sonic's arms. He had just realised something very important.

'Sonic, we're trapped in here! There's no way back out!'

The tomb began to open.

'Oh crikey! The Curse of the Pharaoh's tomb! Wail! We're doomed. I've seen it on video, everyone who enters a tomb like this ends up with 'orrible things happening to them!' Tails yelled. He was getting seriously frantic.

The tomb lid flew open. From the hollow interior, a very heavily bandaged squirrel lumbered out.

'Come to mummy,' the thing crooned in a distressingly Sally Acorn-like voice.

'Sally! Oh no!' Tails cried out. 'That fiend Robotnik! He's killed our buddy Sally!'

'No. It just looks like her. Like the Count appeared to be just like Joe. It's not really her, it's the monster that Robotnik wants to turn her into,' Sonic said as he edged away from the lumbering thing. The problem was, there just wasn't all that much room for edging awaying. The mummy looked too much like Sally for comfort. The thought that this was what Robotnik wanted to make Sally into was hideously heinous. Somehow, Sonic just couldn't bring himself to attack it. It felt totally wrong attacking something that looked like Sally after a particular accident-prone day, so instead he began to kick over the vases and urns, blocking the mummy's approach. With outstretched arms, fragments of yellowing bandages hanging from them, the grisly-looking thing kept heading remorselessly for them.

'Watch out, Sonic! If they touch you, you get an 'orrible wasting disease!' Tails yelled. 'Ooh! I don't feel well; perhaps I've caught it already! What are we going to do?'

It was at that moment that the jackal-headed statues decided to become animated and lumbered into life themselves. Robotic arms outstretched just like the mummy's, they encircled Sonic and Tails.

The heroes were trapped!

14

THINGS THAT GO BUMP IN THE DAYTIME

A hatch in the floor opened and a sniffling robot emerged into the tomb. The animated robots and the Mummy continued to press forwards. Sonic and Tails took one look at the hatch and decided to make a dive for it. When they did, they found a film crew of robots eagerly waiting underneath.

'First call for make-up, luvvies,' crooned a rather elegant-looking robot with coiffed metallic hair. 'Good scene, good scene, my luvs. Loved the feeling! Exude, exude, that's what the director always said. I thought you were just super, darlings.'

The hatch closed behind them, the mummy and the attacking robots left behind in the tomb. They could hear an angry mummy jumping up and down on the floor above them.

'Oooh, those actresses, they're so temperamental,' the robot said disapprovingly. 'Honestly, give them a bit part and they think they can throw tantrums like real stars. Little madam.'

Sonic and Tails looked at each other in stunned amazement. The degree of bogusness had passed beyond the max and was now accelerating into the depths of the megabogus. After a night without sleep, they began to wonder if they weren't, after all, fast asleep and dreaming – or having a nightmare.

'Do you mind if I just fluff up those spines a little?' said a diminutive robot with a disarming resemblance to one of Robotnik's Coconuts. 'And perhaps a little bit of blusher? Bring out the colour in your cheeks. Ooooh, you do look pale, you know.'

'Of course I do,' Sonic said irritably, pushing away the face puff being shoved at him. 'I've been awake all night, and I'm bushed.'

'Ooooh! You actors, you're all the same. All-night parties and dancing 'til dawn, eh, I shouldn't wonder. You should look after yourself better. Your body is a temple,' the robot said bizarrely.

'Well,' Tails said in a moment of inspiration, 'the thing is, we need relaxation. Outside the castle.'

'Outside the castle?' the film crew said as one. They were clearly suspicious.

'Ah. No, not exactly outside the castle,' Tails said hurriedly. 'We have a scene to retake with the headless horseman. In the coach-house,' he explained. 'We could relax and get some fresh air. That would make us look much better,' he concluded hopefully.

'Oh, why didn't you say so?' said the Slicer-like robot with the improbable metal coiffure. 'Well, perhaps we could arrange that. But right now you're wanted at the Grey Tower, dears. The Director is quite adamant. And you know what happens when you keep old Bossy Britches waiting.'

Sonic and Tails groaned. They were desperately tired and they needed to find somewhere safe to sleep, and

Castle Robotnik certainly wasn't safe. If only they had noticed that the robot mentioned a director. The other film crew had mentioned the producer. But, then, after a night without sleep hedgehogs and foxes aren't at their most observant and what the heck, directors and producers are both dweebs anyway.

'We've been working more hours than we're supposed to, it's against the rules of the actor's union,' Sonic pleaded. 'We need our rest!'

'I'm sorry, luvs,' the Slicer said with a steely edge to its voice, 'but if we don't bring in this movie on time we're scrap metal and you're just a pair of has-beens without any future in this tinseltown city. So let's be little professionals, shall we? Just the scenes in the Grey Tower to do and then you can have your quality time, luvvies. And remember: exude!'

'I wish I had the energy to stomp these totally annoying nerds,' Sonic whispered to Tails. 'I suppose we'll have to go along with them, though. The weird thing is, this doesn't feel like Robotnik is behind it. If he was, and he knew how exhausted we are, he'd send in a bunch of robots to attack us and finish us off, not to do this.'

Tails nodded. It puzzled him too. He pulled his paws out of his pockets, realising for the first time in a while that he was still wearing the dinner jacket he'd put on to dine with the Count.

'I've still got some entrées left,' he said. 'Some nuts and nachos.'

'Why didn't you say so before?' Sonic beamed. 'Right on or what? Let's go and sort out this bogus Grey Tower nonsense, dude.'

'Make-up first,' the robot insisted. 'Must look your best for the big scenes, you know.'

Sonic took one look at the face puff and scowled.

*   *   *

Robotnik was beside himself with rage. He jumped up and down and banged his fists on the consoles. He looked like a huge wobbly yo-yo in a white coat.

'Pah! That hateful hedgehog has escaped again! What are those robots doing? Where did they come from? Spielbot, is that your film crew?' he eggsploded.

'Certainly not!' Spielbot sniffed huffily. 'My fine team of expert robot technicians are in the Grey Tower itself, just in case those animals survive long enough to get there.'

Eggor kept quiet. His plan hadn't worked out at all well. The Master was angry and that was bad news. Eggstraordinarily enough, Robotnik didn't ask him about the second film crew. Part of Eggor was relieved, but part of him was just a little bit annoyed too. He was supposed to be the Director, after all.

'Find them and have them melted down for scrap,' the lunatic scientific genius ordered Eggor. 'Twice.'

Eggor really didn't understand what was going on. On the one hand, Robotnik wanted to make his movie, with its great climatic scene atop the Grey Tower, and that meant that Sonic and Tails had to survive long enough to get there. But when Sonic and Tails were trapped somewhere else in the castle, Robotnik seemed to want to destroy them if he had the chance. It didn't seem to make sense, unless . . .

The Master is confused himself, Eggor realised. He's not certain what he wants. Or perhaps it's just the eggscitement of the moment when the animals are backed into a corner which temporarily overcomes him. But, either way, he is not being entirely *logical*.

That troubled Eggor deeply. Obviously Robotnik was completely mad, but being illogical was something a scientist really shouldn't be. Deranged, yes, but illogical . . .

Eggor shivered.

*   *   *

'Well, maybe just one more quick shine on my sneakers,' said Sonic, relaxing in his chair. The shoe-buffing robot frantically rubbed harder with its cleaning cloth. 'Don't have any pizza at all, do you dude?'

'Tut, tut,' the coiffured robot said. 'No time for meals, luvvie. Anyway, you'll probably bring it back up in the first scene and we can't have that. Look terrified, please, but definitely no pizza-pebbledashing of the walls. Catering will be along later to take your lunch order.'

Tails proudly inspected his newly fluffed tails, using an especially shiny chrome robot as a mirror. He thought he looked really cool. Even his dinner jacket had been cleaned.

'Tell me more about this Grey Tower,' Sonic asked. 'Like, what are we expected to do, exactly?'

The robot in charge looked suspicious again. 'What do you mean? Haven't you read the script? Are you sure you are in this scene?' Other robots began to circle round the animals, looking threatening.

'Oh, right on, make-up dudes. It's just that even the biggest megastars can do with a quick refresher, right? What I meant was, um . . .' Sonic tried to think himself out of trouble. Bad move.

'Yes?' said the robot, still a little uncertain.

'I meant, like, we need your expert guidance on the best scenes to, um, exude in. Give us your creative input,' the hedgehog finished, using one of the gibberish phrases he'd picked up from videos about movie-makers. The robot seemed much more satisfied by that. It preened itself a little, and began to tell Sonic and Tails what to expect from the first two scenes. The friends shot each other worried looks when they found out.

As the robots guided them along the labyrinthine passages to the Grey Tower, Sonic whispered to his friend. 'We could stomp them. I feel a bit better after that sit-down,' the hedgehog growled softly.

'I don't. I'm still exhausted. And even if we do stomp them, we'd still be trapped. We don't know any way out of the castle. Maybe there's one in the Grey Tower, and we really need to find it if it's there. We've got to find somewhere safe to get some food and sleep, and there isn't going to be anywhere safe in here.'

Sonic sighed. Tails was right and he knew it, because he was fatigued too. Thing was, he didn't like not being able to stomp these wretched robots into junk. He tapped the floor with his foot, irked, as a Coconut stopped at a wall panel beside a pair of metal doors and keyed in some entry codes. The doors swished open to reveal an elevator room beyond.

'Top floor, luvvies, and then straight through to the top,' the robot leader said. 'And, don't forget –'

'Yes, I know,' Sonic sighed. 'Exude, exude.' The moment the robot turned away, he looked at Tails and, putting two fingers up to his mouth, made 'I want to puke' signs. He stepped into the elevator with Tails and pressed the top button. Within seconds, they were atop the Grey Tower, and they stepped out into a bare room without any windows. There was still no way out that they could see.

'Okay, here goes, dude,' Sonic said, breathing heavily. 'Let's get this turkey on the road.' He crossed the room and opened the door on the far side. As he'd been told, there was a long monorail spiralling crazily downwards to the bottom of the tower, and a single open carriage for riding down it. Because the monorail was built in a wide spiral around a central stone pillar, they couldn't see what lay below them, but they got into the carriage anyway.

'Going down,' sneered an automated robotic voice. 'Welcome to the helter-skelter. Heh heh!'

The carriage gave a lunge forward and then accelerated more smoothly. Soon it was hurtling down faster than a robot Sonic had just kicked off a rooftop.

'I'm getting dizzy,' Tails whined. 'My brain hurts. Awwuurgggh!' The carriage started rocking from side to side and they had to hold on with their paws. Tails was going a nasty shade of puce and his white-knuckled paws gripped the side of the carriage for dear life. The helter-skelter suddenly hit the bottom of the descent and almost threw them out. Then it lurched forward again, through a huge archway with the words 'GHOST TRAIN' painted in large, spooky letters above it.

'Bogus or what?' Sonic said irritably. 'Ghosts and ghoulies, huh? Let me at 'em!' The carriage shot forwards.

It was very, very dark inside the ghost-train tunnel. They could hear the sound of lapping water all around them, so it was plainly too big a risk to jump out of the carriage and look for a way out at random. Luminous painted skeletons and leering pumpkin faces flew at them from all sides, almost colliding with them.

'Yikes! It's getting scary,' Tails whimpered. He really didn't like this kind of thing at all.

'Huh! It's all fake,' Sonic repeated as if trying to persuade himself too that was true. It wasn't nice down here at all and it was too dark to see anything, which really cheesed him off.

The carriage lumbered to a halt, tipped over sideways, and dumped them out on to solid ground. The sound of flowing water was a little way behind them now, and a dim light came from flickering candles set in brackets along the walls. It was very quiet here, and dirty cobwebs and dust lurked in all the corners and crevices of the stone passageways. It was more than a little spooky.

'Let's get moving. Keep checking the walls. There may be something hidden, like that revolving bookcase door you found in the library or that secret door behind the Pharaoh's statue,' Sonic advised; he'd seen this sort of movie hundreds of times. 'There's got to be a way out

somewhere. If Robotnik has put traps or robots into this place, dude, he must have got in to do it. That means there must be a way in – and a way out.'

'Unless he bricked it up on the way out,' Tails lamented. 'Perhaps we'll end up in one of those stories about people bring bricked up alive. Oh, that's too gross!'

A faint wail came from the distance. The fur along Tails's spine raised up a little and he almost looked like Sonic in the spiny department.

'What was that?' he whispered.

'We know what it was. It's just a special effect,' Sonic scoffed. 'Real ghosts don't exist. Everyone knows that.'

A luminous phantasm drifted into sight around the corner they'd left behind them. It looked like a venerable, white-haired old human, and a second ghost, which looked like a large green blob, bobbed along happily behind it. The man looked awfully convincing for a special effect.

'Woe is me,' the figure lamented. 'Condemned to haunt this ghastly castle all my days!'

'We're not scared. We know you're a bogus special effect,' Sonic challenged it. Tails cowered behind him to add extra substance to his words.

'You disrespectful little toe-rag,' the man snarled. 'I used to be one of the finest actors of my generation until that horrible, horrible man disposed of me. Now I have to haunt this awful place!'

'Disposed of you?' Tails was wide-eyed.

'That's what I said, didn't I? Are you deaf or something?' the ghost scowled and then let out another horrible wail.

'I wish you wouldn't do that,' Tails said. 'I've got a bit of a headache already.'

'Headache? Headache? Is that all? Listen, you furry dweeb, I'm condemned to haunt here for all eternity in endless suffering and misery. You have no idea what that's like.'

'Is it a bit like having the Count's poetry read to you every day for the rest of your life?' Tails asked helpfully.

'Worse. And it goes on forever. Long after you've scoffed your last pizza I'll be trapped here still, with no one for company. Oh woe is me!' The ghost wailed again. It really was a scary and distressing sound. Then the ghost's expression changed. 'But I suppose I could have some company now!'

'What do you mean?' Sonic asked suspiciously.

'I mean, if you became ghosts then I'd have you to talk to. You're not much, let's face it, but I suppose you'd be better than nothing.'

'But we aren't ghosts. No one becomes a ghost unless . . . unless . . . ,' Tails said, cowering even more.

'Right. Unless they're DEAD!' The ghost turned to his blobby green companion, which had until now said nothing. 'Udolpho: slime them, boy!'

Our heroes turned as one and fled as a huge glob of green slime slammed into the wall at their backs. They could hear the fizzing of powerful acid dissolving the stone behind them even as they ran like crazy.

'What are we gonna do? We can't stomp that. If we get hit by that yucky stuff, it'll make Mega Mack look like sodapop,' Tails yelped breathlessly as they ran at full pelt.

Behind them, the green blob flew through the air, spraying slime all around it. What was even worse was that they were now running ankle-deep in gooey sludge. It was a bit like the Mega Mack of the Chemical Plant Zone, or at least it smelt like it, but fortunately it didn't make them stick to the floor. And it didn't threaten to dissolve them like the slime the green blob was spraying around. But it did make Sonic's freshly cleaned sneakers slimy, and he absolutely hated that.

Sonic spotted a metal door ahead of him and, as he got closer to it, his sneakers burning up the ground, he saw the

sign on it: 'SPECIAL EFFECTS'. He smashed into the door
and knocked it down. There was a huge clutter of equipment and props stored in the room, and right in the centre
on a large table was a very complicated and weird-looking
machine.

'Whatcha gonna do?' Sonic said. 'Call Slimebusters!'

Of course, it had helped to have a spied a manual
bearing the title *Ghost Neutralising with the Mark 12 Neu-
tronic Slime Imploder* on the table beside the machine.
Desperately, he picked it up and began looking at the
diagrams on the first pages. Sonic was not good at working
out the details of fabulously complicated scientific
machinery. The green spectre appeared at the doorway.

'Keep back!' Sonic yelled, pointing something that
looked very like one of those vacuum-cleaner attachments
you use for cleaning the stairs at the hovering horror. 'Or
else you're slime history, ghostly blob-type dude.'

The green blob wobbled up and down uncertainly.

'Now, why don't we just talk about this like reasonable
guys?' Tails said hopefully. The blob sneakily advanced a
metre or so, until Sonic held out the vacuum cleaner again
and flicked a switch on the machine. It began to hum. The
blob retreated.

'Udolpho!' a voice came from somewhere outside the
room, getting closer. 'I said slime them!'

The blob began to expand. It was winding itself up for a
real mega slime-out. Sonic pressed every button and
switch he could find and hoped for the best. A ray of pearly
light shot out from the attachment he was holding – and hit
the blob!

The result was totally awesome, and plainly very
expensive.

The blob imploded. It collapsed in on itself until it was
nothing more than a single pinpoint of green light and then
it was sucked into the white light and drawn into the

machine. Sonic felt the metal tube he was holding getting very hot, and the machine began to smoke rather worryingly. Then it began to hum, a grating buzz which got louder and louder.

'It's going to explode, Sonic!' Tails yelped. 'Let's scarper!'

Just then, the white-haired ghost appeared in the doorway. He looked a bit miffed, to say the least.

'Yes, run you wretches,' he leered. 'Come to me!' He stretched out his ghostly arms. The pair shrank back. The machine howled. Sonic kept on pressing switches and pulled a large red lever which had a sign above it which read *'Do Not Pull Under Any Circumstances'*.

The machine fell apart, but as it did so every bit of weird energy stored inside in it discharged itself through the tube Sonic was still holding. The recoil was so tremendous that the hedgehog was flung back against the far wall, knocking him into the middle of next week. A huge white blob of supernatural (or perhaps special effect-ual!) force screamed out across the room, blew apart the ghost standing in the doorway, and hit the wall of the passage outside. The stonework dissolved, and kept on dissolving. As Tails stared at it, he saw a tunnel being burned right through the stone – and at the end of it there was daylight!

Tails helped the stunned hedgehog to his feet. Sonic tottered a little unsteadily across the room, still seeing tiny green blob-things circling round his head from the force of hitting the wall.

'I think we just found a way out!' Tails squeaked excitedly.

'Yeah, like, totally! Let's grab a souvenir or too before we go,' the hedgehog growled, his senses slowly returning to him. 'I can think of someone who just might be able to tell us something about them.'

15

WHAT'S IN THE BOX, DUDE?

'We're going to be melted down for scrap,' Spielbot groaned. 'I'll never get to make my best movies now. Blast that hedgehog!'

'I'm not so sure,' Eggor said slowly. He'd been doing some more research on Robotnik's monster atop the Great Tower and now he thought he understood a bit better. 'The Master did get something he wanted.'

'What? They escaped,' the assistant director pointed out.

'Yes. But they will be back. And we have plenty of footage of them being eggstremely frightened,' Eggor replied.

'Great. What good's that going to do?'

'Well, it's like this . . .'

Sonic rubbed his eyes. He'd been asleep for hours and hours, and boy, had he needed his beauty sleep! All the excitement of the castle had drained him of energy. Now it was time to stuff his face!

Tails was still dozing when the smell of pizza made his nose twitch. Within seconds he was wide awake and scuttling downstairs, only to find a hedgehog sat before an empty pizza box and with cheesy bits all over his paws. Fortunately, there were plenty more pizza boxes piled up beside him and they didn't look as if they were empty at all. Ten minutes later, after a hideously high-speed pork-out, the pals rubbed their stomachs and looked a lot happier with life.

There was a knock at the door. Tails grabbed his cloves of garlic and stood defensively before the door, his tail-tips wagging ever so slightly.

'It's only me,' came a squirrelly voice.

'The mummy?' Tails said suspiciously. It hasn't been so long since they'd escaped and he wasn't taking any chances.

'What do you mean?' the voice got more irked. 'It's Sally! Open the door, you silly fox! Where's Sonic? Are you okay?'

The hedgehog opened the door. Sally Acorn and his other friends were standing outside. He was incredibly relieved to see them all.

'Come on in,' he said. 'I'm afraid we just finished the pizzas, dudes.'

'So what else is new?' laughed Johnny Lightfoot.

'Well then, I guess you won't be wanting any of these,' Joe Sushi chuckled. Sonic could see now that he was carrying a pile of pizza boxes almost as tall as he was.

'Well, there's always room for some more,' the hedgehog said hungrily. As he scoffed, he began to tell them all the story of their exploits inside the castle. When he'd finished, his audience looked extremely worried.

'So Robotnik wants to turn us all into monsters? That's just blooming typical,' Joe growled.

'If he can do it!' Johnny scoffed.

'But he can! He may have already started!' Sally exclaimed. 'What about Porker?' They looked frightened then.

'How is he?' Sonic asked anxiously.

'Well,' Sally said slowly, 'he's a bit pale.'

'Yes, and?' Tails asked, not really wanting to know the worst.

'And he sleeps in the daytime.'

'Oh.' That didn't sound too good.

'And he can't even face the thought of garlic pizza.'

'Oh dear.' It wasn't much of a reply but it was all Tails could think of to say.

'He's also got weird little warts growing all over him,' Johnny said.

'Oh, gross!' Tails said disgustedly.

'We didn't meet anything like Porker in the castle,' Sonic said thoughtfully. 'So I don't know what Robotnik might be turning him into. It doesn't sound like just being a vampire, does it? Joe didn't have any warts. Oops! I mean the Count, of course; sorry Joe.'

'We'll have to find out if we're going to help him,' Tails pointed out. 'That means going back . . . *in there!*

Suddenly the others all looked as if they'd just remembered a very urgent appointment somewhere else.

'And we won't be able just to go in and smash the place up,' Tails said sadly. 'We'll have to find out exactly what's been done to Porker, and how to reverse it.'

'We have a start,' Sonic said angrily. 'Let's hit the Emerald Hill Zone. We've got something to show Mickey. While we're gone, though, I think you guys had better stock up with lots of food and keep inside. Bar your doors and don't let anyone you don't know come in.'

'But if Robotnik wants to turn us into monsters, and if he's already started with Porker, then we might not be safe even letting in someone we do know,' Tux pointed out.

'They might have been monsterfied' He paused, his little beak trying not to say what he was thinking, and failing badly. 'I mean, um, how do we know you aren't monsters?'

'You don't,' Tails said grimly. 'But if you see a wolf with two tails and teeth as large as Joe's fangs, then you can really start worrying! All right?' That made everyone quiet.

'Let's go,' Sonic said, brimming with vitality after his massive eating binge. Boundless energy had returned to him, and he wanted to get out there and jolly well do something after all this talking. At least a good run to the Emerald Hill Zone would burn off some of his extra zip, even if there might be more talking to do there. With Tails in hot pursuit, he raced out of the door, pausing only to shove a few dozen packs of crisps, nuts and nachos into a bag for along the way.

Behind them, Tails and Sonic left a collection of very uncertain friends.

'I guess he's right. We'll just have to barricade ourselves in,' Tux sighed. 'How annoying. I need my fresh fish! It isn't the same out of the freezer.'

'Well, I don't know,' Sally said crossly. 'We can't expect Sonic and Tails to do absolutely everything while we just sit here like total wimps. I have a Plan.'

They huddled around her to hear the details.

Because they had snoozed all day, it was night time when Sonic and Tails sped into the Emerald Hill Zone. The night was dark and clear. There wasn't anything in the way of thunder, lightning, raindrops or that kind of thing. They even heard the distant hoot of an owl which had cautiously crept back to the Green Hill Zone after having heard encouraging weather reports on the TV. They ignored it and just kept on going. Eventually, they reached a familiar hut, and crept inside.

'Wake up, Mickey! This is important!' Sonic yelled,

shaking the snoozing monkey's shoulders.

'Eh, Whassup? I never touched that hooky gear, guv-nor, on me old gran's life! I sw–oh, it's you blokes,' Mickey said, trying to focus his eyes on the over-excited hedgehog.

'You know about electrical equipment and machines and stuff, don't you?' Sonic said, waving an open pack of dry-roasted peanuts under the confused monkey's nose. 'We need some help. Come on, wake up!'

'I've only just got off to sleep,' Mickey complained. 'I haven't been kipping well lately, what with all this bad weather keeping me awake. Go 'way. Gertcha!'

'Shan't!' Tails replied. 'If you don't help us, Robotnik's going to turn you into a monster too!'

The monkey groaned and yawned as he stretched his arms out. He had bags under his eyes big enough to carry a pizza box home in.

'Well, look, I'm tired and I'm not going to be at my best,' he said defensively.

'There's no time to waste. Now, what can you tell us about this?' Sonic said firmly, thrusting the small machine he'd taken from the castle into the bleary-eyed monkey's face.

'Gimme a chance,' the tired monkey protested. 'Why does it matter anyway?' He got out of his bed, scratching at his long white nightshirt.

'It's from Robotnik's castle. I think it's important,' Sonic said.

'Oh well then,' Mickey sighed, rummaging through his tool boxes. 'Why didn't you chumps say so? Let's fire it up and see what it does.' Tails and Sonic sat down and began their patient wait.

After two hours of clipping on electrodes and clips, testing the box with a variety of strange-looking equipment of his own devising, Mickey was still hard at work.

'Where did you get all that stuff?' Tails asked, looking at the oscilloscopes and pulse generators and all the rest of the junk.

'Made a killing selling coconuts to the Roaming Romans,' Mickey replied. 'Used the money to buy up some bankrupt stock in the Metropolis Zone. Capone brokered the deal.' Sonic bristled at the mention of the rat. 'Look, I got six boxes of electric hair curlers if you want to buy one for Sally. Only cost you ten pizzas. You could do with one for your spines, matey.'

'I do NOT want my spines curly,' the hedgehog protested angrily.

'You'd look super with a light perm, luvvie,' the monkey sniggered. Tails regretted recounting their exploits to him now. He had a horrible feeling that the mischievous monkeys of the Emerald Hill Zone were going to be calling them annoying names for a long, long time.

'I like the way I am, thanks all the same,' Sonic growled.

Mickey sat back and surveyed his work. 'Well, chums, I've put your box through all the tests I can think of,' he sighed.

'And?' Tails enquired.

'Well, it's Weird Science basically,' the monkey apologised. 'It's some kind of energy-storing and transforming device. Something to do with biological energy.'

'Like in living things?' Tails offered.

'You putting in an entry for the Mobius Prize for Stating the Bleeding Obvious or what?' Mickey sniggered. 'I said it was about biology, didn't I? Not much biology in rocks and stones, you dozy fox.'

'Well if you're so clever, how come you can't tell us what it is?' Tails replied. Mickey looked a little taken aback by that.

'Can we use it?' Sonic asked.

'Weeeelll,' Mickey hesitated, 'you could. It would be

incredibly dangerous, though. There's absolutely no way of knowing what might happen.'

'Could it be the thing Robotnik is using for turning animals into monsters?' Tails asked him.

'It might be,' Mickey said slowly, 'but Robotnik must have a better way of doing it hidden somewhere else in the castle. He's not going to leave his most vital machine just lying around in a special effects store, is he?'

'Unless it's a prototype,' Tails offered. 'Remember that Mark I Transmogrifier thingie we found in his old laboratory in the Scrap Brain Zone before? When he was turning everyone into household objects?'

'Well, that's enough nattering. We've got to split,' Sonic said, tapping his foot on the ground impatiently. 'How do you use the machine, exactly?'

'You just push the button marked "On",' Mickey replied evenly.

'Oh. Didn't think of that,' Sonic said rather grumpily.

'But don't do it except in an absolute emergency. Like, if you're just about to be ripped into tiny, bloody pieces and gobbets of flesh by some hideous monster,' Mickey added with relish.

'Thanks,' Tails replied dryly.

'And it won't be any good against robots either,' Mickey said.

'Terrific,' Tails concluded.

'And stand well back,' Mickey chuckled.

'Yes, well, thanks for the help, dude, but now we super-heroes must dash,' Sonic finished, hurrying Tails along with him. 'We have a madman and a castle still half-full of monsters to demolish. Catch you later. Cowabunga, dude!'

The hedgehog and fox dashed away through the palm trees, leaving an exhausted monkey to go back to dreaming of bananas the size of marrows.

16

THE TOWER OF POWER

Old Robotnik had seriously upgraded the defences of his fortress in the Scrap Brain Zone by the time Sonic and Tails arrived there once more. A squadron of Buzzers prowled the skies above a small army of Grabbers patrolling the ruined, blasted ground around the castle.

'Huh! Badniks,' Sonic growled. 'Nothing we can't handle, though. There can't be more than a couple of hundred of them. Piece of cake.'

'Don't mind if I do. Oh, sorry Sonic; I see what you mean.' Tails was studying the castle. After their long sojourn with Mickey, dawn was just breaking and this was the first time they had actually seen the building in daylight.

'Hmmm,' Tails pondered. 'There's the Black Tower, and next to it is the Grey Tower, then the White Tower where our so-called "guest room" was. There's the really big tower in the middle – that's got to be where Robotnik's master laboratory is. We have a choice, buddy.'

'Yeah. Do we smash it all down now or go on talking?' Sonic replied. He was itching to bounce some badniks.

'No, wait a second. I reckon that Robotnik has stationed lots more badniks inside those parts of the castle we know about, in case we return. That would be the sensible thing to do.'

'So what? Let's get smashing!' Sonic was deep in the throes of one of his fits of over-enthusiasm.

'Chill out! Why don't we try to take the one way in through a part of the castle we haven't been into yet? Perhaps there will be fewer badniks there. Then it'll be easier to get into the big tower in the centre, and find out if Porker can be cured.'

'I guess it makes bodaciously good sense. Now can I please go and bounce some heinous badniks?' Sonic pleaded.

'Oh, go on then. Groovy, yeah, but let's head for that fourth, funny-looking tower at the back there. The one with the big metal thing on top of it. That's the one place we haven't been, so there's a better chance of it being unguarded.'

Sonic studied the gleaming metal rig perched right on top of the tower, and tried to figure out what it might be.

'Robotnik can't be drilling for oil, can he?'

'Don't think so,' Tails figured. 'We'll find out what's there when we get in. Hey! Come back! Okay then, don't come back. Wait for me!'

The first of an unsuspecting unit of Grabbers was just about to get smashed to smithereens as a pair of spinning, whizzing superdudes hit full throttle. Leaving a trial of smashed robots behind him, Sonic the hedgehog, closely followed by a puffing Tails, returned to Castle Robotnik.

Not for the first time, Eggor was worried. His plan for using the spare robot film unit to shoot some extra scenes which he, as director, might be able to use in the final cut of the *Castle Robotnik* movie hadn't worked out too well. The robots had saved Sonic and Tails from the mummy in the Black Tower and Dr Robotnik was not pleased about that at all. He had instructed Eggor to find out what had gone wrong with their programming and have the robot responsible melted down for scrap. Since that robot was Eggor himself, he was *seriously* worried. He had to shift the blame somehow.

He accessed all the data he could get from the computer banks on the plans for the film crew in the past. He was alone in the laboratory, since that annoying Spielbot had gone off to take part in some interview Radio Robotnik was making for broadcast all over Mobius, so he could work without being seen by anyone important. Finally, after much searching through the data files, Eggor found what he was looking for: the set of the last Spielbot movie the robotic film crew had worked on and despatched them to it, with instructions to await events.

With any luck, his robotic brain figured, I can ensure that irksome assistant director gets the blame instead of me. I was only obeying my Self-Preservation Circuits, after all. Yes, I'm sure that's acceptable.

'Look! There's a way in, a door,' Tails gasped as he drew alongside Sonic. Buzzers were swarming from the top of the tower and, for every one the superheroes bounced and crashed, another two flew down to the attack. 'Let's get away from these nasty badniks!'

Sonic smashed down the door and hurriedly looked around for something else to smash. He was slightly miffed to find that Tails's guesstimate had been right and the place appeared to be unguarded after all.

'Don't forget, we're here to find out what's going on before we smash everything in sight,' Tails said in best party-pooper vein. 'We've got to find a cure for Porker, right? And stop anyone else being turned into a monster!'

'Right-o,' Sonic sighed. 'Hey, you know, this place looks familiar.'

Tails looked around the corridors inside the tower and whistled. 'Yeah, déja vu!'

There was a maze of plushly carpeted passages, elevators, and doors with red lights winking alongside them and a sign reading 'ON THE AIR' over one of them.

'Just like a radio station, right? That's what the metal rig on top of the tower must have been: a radio transmitter. I bet you a double-cheese deep pan to a peanut this is where that dastardly madman has shifted Radio Robotnik to.' The hedgehog did his best to lean the door up on its hinges to keep the Buzzers out. The noise of their angry swarming was getting louder and louder outside.

'Let's just hide somewhere for a minute until they've gone away,' Tails said reasonably. They pushed open the first door they found and leapt into a hospitality room.

'Hey, this must be a hospitality room,' Sonic said brightly.

'What's a hospitality room? Tails asked.

'It's where overpaid radio hacks drink themselves stupid and fawn over over-rated and under-talented guests who aren't worth getting on to TV,' Sonic sniggered.

'How do you know so much about it?' Tails asked suspiciously.

'Oh, well, erm, I'm the hero. I know lots of trivial stuff, honest,' Sonic covered hastily. 'But that's not what's important right now, dude. There are two things that matter most radically here. First, it's probably safe to hide here.'

'Well, that's cool,' the fox said, relieved.

'And even more importantly, if you open those cupboards right there you will most indisputably find enormous amounts of ultra-tasty snack-type nibbles. Gong! It's lunch time!'

One brief, face-filling, stomach-bloating intermission

later, Sonic sprawled out, porked to the gills, on one of the luxurious armchairs.

'This is the life, my little foxy buddy. I could get used to this. Perhaps I ought to become a guest on radio shows full-time,' he sighed.

'I don't think so,' Tails said dubiously. He was anxious when Sonic got close to any kind of broadcasting studio. The hedgehog's liking for being famous often led him to get into scrapes he shouldn't.

'What is on the radio, anyway?' Sonic wondered. He flicked on the radio on the table. It didn't need tuning in, since the only station it broadcast was Radio Robotnik, of course.

'. . . and today, on *Movie World*, we have Spielbot S as our guest. World-famous movie-maker for Trundlin' Robot Productions, Spielbot S is here to tell us about his art.'

Sonic groaned. 'Borrr-ing!'

'And also about the movie he is currently working on, *Castle Robotnik.*'

Sonic perked up his ears.

'Mr Spielbot, if I may call you that . . .'

'Please do,' came a smarmy robotic voice.

'I understand that this is your biggest-budget picture yet.'

'Indeed. The executive producer, none other than Dr Robotnik himself, has insisted on the very highest production and creative values for this timely project.'

'Why can't they speak properly?' Tails moaned. The smooth robot's voice droned on.

'Quite literally no expense has been spared for the special effects in this movie which is the best I have ever worked on, and I mean that most honestly and sincerely.'

Sonic felt faintly nauseous.

'Can you tell us about the storyline?' the interviewer asked.

'Well, listeners, it concerns the brave attempts of a truly heroic scientist to push back the boundaries of knowledge into hitherto uncharted areas, to boldly go where no brain has gone before . . .'

'Wait a minute, I've heard that line before,' Sonic thought aloud.

'. . . and the attempts of a pair of dangerous evil pinko subversive guerrilla terrorists to prevent his eggsceptional eggsperimental work from coming to fruition. Fortunately, they are defeated – after a series of dangerous, violent action scenes unparalleled in Mobius movie history – by the scientist's master creation.'

'Now that sounds interesting,' Tails growled. 'What's that, I wonder? Something 'orribly 'orrible, I bet.'

'Huh,' Sonic sneered, 'this is bogus! Gorillas indeed! Anyone can see I'm a hedgehog and you're a fox.' Tails hushed him; he wanted to hear whether Spielbot was going to tell them what the creation was.

'And just what is that creation?' the interviewer probed. Tails and Sonic listened intently. They were to be disappointed.

'I'm afraid I can't reveal that,' Spielbot said, with just the right hint of 'I know you want to know, so I'll pretend that I'd really like to tell you' in his voice.

'Bogus or what?' Sonic said sadly.

'Well, perhaps listeners to fab, groovy Radio Robotnik would like to be reminded about some of your previous excellent movies before they phone in. Yes, don't forget, all you eager listeners, you can call us on 555-ROBOTNIK with your questions for our world-famous guest. And the lines are open now!'

.'What was that number?' Sonic perked up.

'That number again: just dial 555-ROBOTNIK to get through live on the air, right here on Radio Robotnik where you are listening to Robot Robotson talking to Spielbot S about his career in movies,' the radio voice obliged.

'I have an idea,' Sonic smirked.

Tails got worried immediately. The hedgehog had already picked up the phone conveniently sitting on the table before him, and was keying in the dialling code with a determined grin on his face. He got through and was put on hold for the first call by a robotic secretary.

'And we have our first caller on the line,' the presenter said happily a couple of minutes later when the Spielbot had finished his account of his long and glorious Eggscar-winning career. 'What is your name, sir?'

'Hello, Brian, first-time caller! I'm, um, Ronald Rat from the Metropolis Zone,' Sonic lied in a squeaky voice, apparently doing his best to imitate a rodent. 'I used to be on breakfast telly, remember?'

'Er, no, not really,' the interviewer said slightly worriedly.

'It was a while ago,' Sonic said. 'Anyway, Brian, I'd like to congratulate Mr Spielbot on providing us, the humble general public, with his wonderful movies for so many years, which have given us all a radically huge amount of pleasure. Like, totally mega-awesome or what?'

'Thank you so much,' said Spielbot S. He was audibly preening itself.

'Now, am I right in thinking that a lot of your movies have featured weird and strange alien species?' Sonic queried.

'Oh yes, indeed,' Spielbot said a little uncertainly. He clearly wasn't sure what question was coming next.

'I just wondered if you'd been involved on any research into aliens and monsters,' Sonic squeaked on. 'As background research for your latest, radically bodacious movie epic.'

'Erm,' stuttered Spielbot. 'What do you mean, caller? I mean, Mr Rat?'

'The monsters in your new movie. Have you been involved in scientific research for their creation, and what can you tell us about it?' Sonic was fishing for information. There was a long silence.

'I didn't say there were any monsters in my new movie,' Spielbot said suspiciously. Tails's eyes grew wide; uh-oh!

'I'm sure you did,' Sonic said, forgetting to use his squeaky voice. He couldn't remember himself now.

'I most certainly did not!' Spielbot retorted with more certainty. 'I said the movie was about heroic scientific research, and I did not mention monsters at all. Just where are you calling from, Mr Rat?'

'Put the phone down, Sonic!' Tails yelled. 'They're going to trace the call!' Unfortunately, he shouted loud enough to be heard over the phone.

'Too right we are,' Robot Robotson snarled angrily, his usual fawning cool terminally stripped away. 'You're about to become an ex-rat, Ronald. Or should that be an ex-hedgehog?!'

Sonic slammed down the receiver. 'It seemed like a cool idea. Thought we might learn something,' he pleaded unconvincingly.

'Let's just get out of here,' Tails said grimly. 'I don't want to be an ex-rat. If you know what I mean.'

They fled from the hospitality room, only to find the veritable squadron of Buzzers swarming into the tower through the one exit door. There were so many of them it would surely have been impossible to fight a way through. Sonic thought he could do it, but if anything came from inside the tower – and he was sure something would turn up after his mega-gaffe on the radio phone-in – him and the little guy would be boxed in and attacked from all sides. Even a superbrave supercool megadude like, well, you know who, didn't fancy that prospect. With Tails right behind him, he dashed off further into the depths of the tower.

For some reason, the Buzzers didn't follow them. Sonic

guessed they were staying to guard the way out. But up ahead he could see rows of Bomb Bots and Ball Hogs trundling towards them. There was a seriously large number of them, and their expected ETA was any moment n –.

'Yikes!' Tails yelped and hared off down a side passage. Sonic sped after him. He would have loved to smash the Ball Hogs at least, but the unpredictable Bomb Bots were another kettle of badniks entirely. They were really far too dangerous to attack en masse, whatever that meant.

As they tore off down the new passage, they didn't notice that the floor had changed beneath them. Instead of solid ground and plush carpets, the floor was made of a cellular matrix. It was something of a surprise, then, when, five metres along, it just fell in on itself, dumping them down into a wholly dark pit beneath the passage. Thankfully unhurt by the fall, they got to their feet and gazed unhappily up at around a hundred badniks who had gathered around the top of the pit and were peering down at the pair with horribly eager looks on their metal faces. Rather than take on so many, Sonic made a dash for the door set in the wall of the pit.

'Welcome,' gloated a monotonous and oily-smooth voice from the room behind the door. 'I'm glad you could make it.'

'Is it, is it – Porker?' Tails gasped. 'Oh lumme, it's the grossest thing I've *ever* seen!!'

17

MARCH OF THE KILLER PIGS

The horror sat bolt upright in a black, throne-like chair, its back as stiff as a steel rod. It wore black all over, so about all they could see of it was its head and its trotters. In appearance it looked very like their piggy pal Porker Lewis, but there were some differences from their buddy which weren't exactly subtle. His head appeared to have a map grid drawn all over it and was entirely bald. Most notable, however, were the pins which protruded from his face and skull all along the grid lines. The pinhead-covered thing leered at them with a sadistic grin and lifted up a strange black box in its trotters as our heroes approached uncertainly. Suddenly, the door slammed behind them, sealing them in this weird room. High on the walls, swivel-mounted cameras twisted to take in the scene from every angle. Sonic and Tails were back in Robotnik's clutches again for sure.

'Like, um, you have a radically unusual appearance, spiky dude,' Sonic said questioningly. 'You're not related to Porker Lewis are you, by any chance? 'Cause he's a cool-dude buddy of ours.'

'Porker Lewis?' the thing said mockingly, its voice halfway between the irritating grinding noise you get off an old door and the growl of a seriously annoyed tiger. 'I don't think so. Oh no.'

'It's just that, um, he's been growing funny little warts where you have those, well, pin things sticking out of your skin. Aren't they painful?' Tails asked.

'Not at all. Oh no,' the thing said casually. It waved one pale trotter and there was a loud bang and a steaming cloud of smoke from right behind them.

'Eek!' Tails cried out and leapt forward to avoid having his twin tails set on fire. 'Hey, mate, that isn't very friendly!'

'I'm not always a very friendly person,' the thing snarled. 'I like making things go bang for no real reason. I'm very good at it too. Oh yes.'

'Who are you?' Sonic asked plainly. He wanted to buy himself some time by talking to this monster so he could look around for ways of escape. To his dismay, though, there wasn't anything obvious on offer. Besides, he didn't want to take too many risks with something that could cause explosions whenever it wanted to.

'My name is Pinhead, but you can call me Pinny. Oh yes,' the thing sniggered. 'I'm a Senileobite.'

'Oh really? And what exactly is, an, um, whatever it was you said just then?' Tails asked hopefully.

'That's not important right now,' Pinny replied, rolling his strange metal box around in his trotters.

'And what's that?' Sonic asked, pointing to the box. 'If I may be so bold to, like, ask?' he added.

'It's called a Dement Configuration. I can turn you into a drooling lunatic with no brains if I wish to, using this. Mind you, that wouldn't be difficult in your case. Oh no,' Pinny said dryly.

Sonic tried to ignore the rather childish insult. But failed. 'Look, thumb-tack features, you bogus porcine pin-

cushion, we're here to find out what's happened to our dear chum Porker, and it looks like he could be turning into something like you. We want to know how something that heinous happens to a regular dude.'

'But Porker's turning into a vampire,' Tails interjected in confusion. 'He can't stand garlic and he's very pale, just like a vampire.'

'Well, I don't like garlic either, and as you can see I'm very pale, but that doesn't make me a vampire,' Pinny said, a little miffed. 'I'm a Senileobite, like I told you. Oh yes.'

'Well then tell us how you become one, and how to stop it, or else I'm gonna bash you one!' Sonic yelled.

It wasn't exactly the right thing to say. The creature rose to his feet and waved a trotter. Another bang came from just behind Sonic and Tails, who both leapt with fright. With a second wave, the spiny pig-thing somehow conjured a huge web of straps and chains which swooped around Sonic and pinned him to the wall.

'Bash me now, you foolish flea-bitten hedgehog,' Pinny snarled. Sonic tried to wriggle free, but stopped trying very quickly when he realised that every movement was making his bonds tighter.

Then the pig-thing raised his box and gave its edges a special secret twist. It switched shape from a box to something more complex, and began to glow with an eerie orange light. The faint smell of fried bacon permeated the room.

Sonic started to wobble and drool. He gurgled a bit and his head hung limply on his chest.

'Sonic? Speak to me, Sonic!' pleaded Tails.

'Coochie-goo,' dribbled Sonic.

Pinny turned to give Tails a stare that said 'Now it's your turn, puny creature', but the little fox was too fast for him. Trademark twin tails spinning, he crashed into the black-clad pinheaded pig-thing and knocked him flying. The strange magic box went spinning from the thing's hands and flew high into the air. It smashed against a wall camera which had been filming the scene, and then it kind of exploded.

Well, no, that's not strictly true. It didn't just go bang; it erupted in a wave of many coloured rays, smoke and loud, eerie, wailing noises. A wave of powerful magical rays sprayed through the entire room, and suddenly Tails was spinning through the air, lazily drifting, unable to control his movements. In the distance he could see Sonic spinning around just as helplessly, freed from the bonds in which the pig-thing had restrained him.

Tails finally figured out where he was when the stars started flying around him. He was in one of the Warps of Confusion which were scattered around Mobius. Somehow, whatever gimmickry had been packed into the – what was it called? – Dement Configuration had projected them into it when it was destroyed. The good news was that there wasn't any sign of Pinny. Bouncing around, he put his paw over his head and hoped for the best. Where he would be dumped out of the Warp, he could only guess.

Tails's head started to go wobbly, following the lead of his stomach, which felt very bad indeed. He saw double, and then triple: there were three drooling blue hedgehogs circling around him. Tails shut his eyes and started yelling, 'There's no place like home! There's no place like home!'

When the fox's senses returned to him, he was lying on the ground on the fringe of some jungle, next to a shattered box and only one drooling Sonic. The only good thing about the scene was that Sonic was covered from head to foot in rings, the powerful energising golden rings which had been scattered throughout Mobius when Dr Ovi Kintobor's ROCC machine had exploded, turning him into the dastardly Dr Ivo Robotnik.

Well, at least they will protect us, wherever we flipping are, Tails thought sadly.

'Coochie-goo,' Sonic dribbled happily. 'Glug, glug. A-gooo!'

Some days, the fox thought, I really ought to stay in bed.

Taking Sonic by one sticky paw and leading him along gently, Tails edged along the margin of the jungle, looking for any source of help, a friend, or even a path to somewhere familiar. He hadn't gone very far when he heard the grunting.

It sounded awful, like some huge ill-mannered beast yelling for its dinner. More urgently, it has to be said, the *Stomp-stomp-stomp* which was coming nearer sounded even more worrying. Tails tried to drag Sonic into the undergrowth at the jungle's edge to hide and so avoid whatever was coming.

The enormous monster lumbered into sight. Tails had never seen anything like it in his life. It looked like a cross between a twenty-metre-tall pig and one of the nastiest dinosaurs he had ever seen on the video or in his many illustrated books. Tails wondered, for one terrifying moment, if it wasn't that Pinhead pig-thing expanded to enormous size by the effects of the exploding Dement Configuration, but it didn't have hundreds of spikes stuck in it, and it didn't really look terribly bright. Thankfully, it also showed no apparent talent for causing mindless, random explosions all over the place.

Looking up at the enormous brute, Tails saw hills far in the distance and a smoking volcano belching out streams of molten lava. Where on Mobius am I? he wondered. Is this Hill Top Zone? It's certainly changed if it is!

'Gurgle gurgle! Dino!' Sonic said loudly. He wriggled out of the fox's grasp and jumped up and down before Tails could grab him and pull him down. Very slowly, the

125

dinosaur-pig's vast head turned to look down at the vanishing blue creature. It looked edible. The creature lumbered forward, demolishing some trees in its path.

'We've got to get away,' Tails yelped to Sonic. The hedgehog burbled happily and refused to budge. Tails grabbed him by the paws and strained with all his might.

'Hee hee! Funny game,' sniggered the hedgehog, resisting with all his might. Since Sonic is bigger, older and ultimately stronger than Tails, the poor fox didn't have much of a chance. He just went red-faced trying to pull Sonic to safety while the hedgehog dug in with his sneakered heels. The monstrous pigosaurus lumbered ever closer, grunting eagerly as it sniffed out its prey.

Tails stood up straight to try to defend his buddy, or just to lure the dinosaur-pig away from him, when a human stumbled into view to his right. At first, Tails thought it was one of Robotnik's droids, because it was clad head to toe in metal. Then he realised it was Sir Norbert.

'Help! I am in need of a brave paladin to save me!' he cried. 'And my poor liege lord buddy, made helpless by foul sorcery!' It was tacky, but it was what he'd seen them say in really naff videos – and it worked.

'Aha!' the man cried happily. 'A Big Scene. At last!' He drew his sword from his scabbard. 'Fresh rashers for breakfast coming up, Gentle Fox!' He raced towards the pig. Tails was deeply glad that the idiot had a clear suicidal urge.

'Drizzle!' came a cry from the knight. 'Bring the enchanted might of the Ebon Staff! This thing is forty hit dice at least!'

Suddenly, an enormous entourage burst through the jungle all round Tails. There were the robots of the film crew, the other actors – and a large gaggle of angry-looking rats in hot pursuit. It was mayhem!

'You come back here and finish that action movie,'

Capone snarled to the directing robot. 'Or else you're scrap, you metal geek.'

'Our orders were to come back to the set of *Jurassic Pork*,' the robot pleaded. 'I am only obeying orders!'

Tails tried to get out of the way of the advancing hordes when a streak of fire from the Ebon Staff of Peaminster flew by, a metre above his hastily cowering head, heading in the general direction of the gigantic pig. A swarm of angry green and yellow parrots rose from the treetops. One of them aimed an accurate missile at Drizzle in retaliation.

'My pointy hat! It's been . . . well, it's absolutely ruined!' moaned the wizard. 'How's that going to look in the movie?'

'I wouldn't worry about that,' the director said. 'We'll just airbrush it out with our video image transforming programs on the computer. It's very sophisticated these days, you know.'

Oh, well that's all right then,' said the wizard happily. 'Okay, get the cameras on me!' The camera crew turned around obediently. The man crouched slightly and did his best to look fierce, rather than the skinny wimp he actually was.

'Eat boiling magical death, you overgrown baconburger!' he screamed and launched another stream of fire from the staff. His aim wasn't any more accurate than the first time around.

The dinosaur-pig was no more than fifty metres away, and grunting very loudly indeed. It licked its lips as it looked down at the conveniently bite-sized snacks ahead of it and stomped every onwards. Tails squeaked.

'Gimme that, you useless dweeb-brain,' snarled Capone, leaping on the wizard and wrestling the staff away from him as half a dozen other rats held him down. 'We should never have let you go anyway!' He fiddled with the staff. 'Hmmm. There's a setting button here. Smoke Puff,

Singe . . . that's no good. Fire Stream. Sounds promising. Aha! Inferno. Now that sounds about right.' He depressed the button, pointed the staff at the gigantic porker and released the button again to fire the staff. Every last drop of gas in it went into the charge. A huge stream of fire sped from it and engulfed everything in front of him. Fortunately, Tails was standing to one side.

When the smoke cleared, what was left on the ground was a baconburger even bigger than anything even Sonic, with his humungous appetite, had imagined in his wildest dreams. Admittedly, it was a bit burnt on the outside, but then you can't have everything. Tails stood and gawped. The rats cheered crazily. The directing robot looked very sad-faced and clanked up to Capone.

'Now, put that in your movie,' Capone said, preening himself. 'Hey, Chloe, you're not doing your fawning-at-my-feet stuff! Get your butt in gear, baby!' The rat moll sighed loudly and flung herself into her adoring routine, batting her eyelashes up at him with the force of a small gale.

'Er, well, luvvie,' the robot began.

'Call me that again and I'll melt you down right now, ya geek,' Capone snarled, pointing the staff at the robot. Tails, in the line of fire behind him, quickly ducked.

'Sorry, lu – er, Your Majesty,' the robot corrected itself hurriedly. 'It's just that we need another take.'

'Another take?' Capone said incredulously. He advanced on the robot.

'I'm afraid the film crew didn't have their cameras loaded,' the robot said, staring down at its metal feet. 'But if you just – '

'How can we do another take, you metal moron?' Capone screamed, jumping up and down from sheer frustration. 'Old Pork Face here is not going to get up and walk around for another shot, is he? It'll take more than a touch of make-up to make him camera-compatible, right?'

'Ah,' the robot stuttered. 'Weeeellll, not exactly. But there are others,' it continued hopefully.

'There are more twenty-metre-tall pigs round here?' the rat said disbelievingly. 'Where do they come from then?'

'They were specially built,' the robot said unhelpfully. 'Something to do with gene splicing and DNA and theme parks and mad scientists and all that kind of thing. Don't ask me, I'm creative, not a scientist. Oh, look, here comes another Velociporker now!'

'This staff is out of juice!' Capone snarled after a hasty test on the single setting. 'Top it up. NOW!'

As a robot minion dumped the contents of its oil sump into the staff, a hitherto silent actor piped up to say his piece.

'Thug wrestle giant pig. Hasta la vista, porky! I'll be back!' With that farewell, he charged off towards the second dino-pig which had just lumbered into view.

Tails had had enough. Sonic seemed to have quietened down a little, and was placidly coochie-cooing to himself. Leading him away from the madness all around them, he began the long trek back to the Green Hill Zone.

Now, he was telling himself, I *think* I know where I am . . .

18

LET ME BORROW YOUR MIND FOR A MINUTE

At the end of the afternoon, an exhausted Tails finally dragged himself back into the Emerald Hill Zone on the last leg of his exhausting journey home. Sonic had shown an infantile and thoroughly annoying dislike for being led along by the hand and had often insisted on stopping and refusing to budge for half an hour while he sniffed some flowers or did something equally un-Sonic-like. Tails's sleep cycles were all messed up, what with sleeping the previous day and having been awake all night, and he was getting very tired and very short-tempered. His mood wasn't improved when, as he was tugging the recalcitrant hedgehog along an overgrown path, a small coconut hit him gently on the back of the head.

'Tee hee,' sniggered a monkey from overhead as it scampered back into its tree. Tails let go of Sonic's hand, raced up the tree and aimed a violent kick at the ape, which it only just avoided. With a howl of fright, it leapt into the next tree. Tails jumped after it and was about to bash it into the middle of next week when he

found himself surrounded by a flock of puzzled bats.

'Hey, fox, chill out. He didn't hurt you,' the bat said, swinging upside down from a branch. 'It was only his curve ball, man.'

Tails cooled down a little. 'I'm sorry, I've had a bad day,' he said.

'Been on the wrong end of a shut-out, yeah? Bummer, man. Happens to the best of us,' the bat said amiably. 'But you know what they say.'

'What do they say?' Tails was too tired to think of a smarter reply.

'Like the coach always says, "It ain't over till the fat lady sings",' the bat repeated happily.

'What does that mean?' Tails said irritably.

'Darned if I know. Coach always was a dweeb,' the bat sniggered. 'Not too many fat ladies up here in these trees, bub. Don't see many playing ball, either.'

'Your blue friend is behaving rather strangely,' another of the bats observed. 'I don't know what he's doing trying to get that rock in his mouth. Is he crazy or something? Man, you wouldn't want him fielding at first base in the Mobius Series.'

'Sort of crazy,' Tails said sadly. 'His brain's been addled by the evil Robotnik. With an 'orrible heinous machine!'

The bats hissed. They weren't very good at hissing, since their vocal chords really weren't designed for it, but they tried their best and if what came out was more like a volley of irate squeaks, well, that wasn't their fault. Tails clambered down the tree to stop Sonic losing all his teeth on his improvised snack.

'Hey man, maybe Mickey can help you,' one of the bats said, swooping down from the tree. 'He's the only guy round here knows about machines. I'll find him for you. Be back before you can call "Strike three!"' With that, it flew off as Tails prised the rock away from Sonic. Within ten minutes, a concerned-looking monkey came puffing up in the distance.

Panting heavily, Mickey strolled up to Tails and Sonic. 'Phew,' he said wiping his brow, 'a bit of the old PT really kills me, me old china. It's not healthy, not good for the old ticker. Righty-ho, what's wrong with old blue bristles then?'

Tails babbled out the whole story and showed Mickey the ruins of the Dement Configuration which he'd thoughtfully picked up and brought with him.

'Well then, Tails, me old cardboard box, I'd better give it the old once-over, lor luvva duck,' the monkey said, turning the strange device over and over in his paws. 'Better bring him with you, bless his cotton socks. Let's see if I can figure out what's been done and whether we can reverse the process.'

They stumped off to Mickey's home. When they got there, Tails was so exhausted that he fell asleep within minutes, leaving a puzzled monkey tinkering with his new toy.

Tails woke with a start as the rosy-fingered Dawn crept into Mickey's house.

'Hello, Dawn,' Mickey said casually. 'Like the nail polish, darling. Thanks for bringing my order over.' He grabbed the burger boxes and waved the girl monkey good-bye as she loped off outside.

'She's just started as delivery person at the pizza and burger store. Really good early-morning service, couldn't ask for better,' the monkey said happily. He grabbed a triple cheeseburger from his box and sunk his teeth into it. 'Yum, yum.'

Tails rubbed the sleep from his eyes with his paws and looked around. Whatever Mickey had been doing, he'd certainly been busy. The contents of the Dement Configuration were laid out everywhere on the floor, connected

by newly soldered wires and lengths of tubing. From this rather weird-looking spread, a couple of what looked suspiciously like metal colanders had been mounted on the wall and were connected to the entire assembly by hastily soldered copper wiring. It didn't exactly look like the work of a brilliant professional craftsman. Meanwhile, Sonic was dozing peacefully in a corner, well out of harm's way. He had one thumb jammed firmly in his mouth, making him look rather sweet.

'Hungry, chum?' Mickey asked cheerily. 'Tuck into something.' He lobbed a box to the eager fox.

'This is very generous of you, Mickey,' Tails said between huge mouthfuls of cheeseburger.

'Think nothing of it. I'm a kindly soul,' the monkey said airily. 'Anyway, it's all gone on Sonic's tab.'

'What did you find out about the box?' the fox said suspiciously. He didn't have too much confidence in the mess of wiring he could see all around him.

'Well, now, it's very interesting,' the monkey said, opening a tattered book with one of his greasy paws while reaching for another burger with the other. 'It's a machine that transforms mental states, don't you know.'

'I sort of guessed that,' Tails said. 'It was fairly obvious, when you consider what happened to him.' He pointed rather guiltily to Sonic.

'Yeah, I know. Real naff up or what? He was a blooming pest until he went to sleep. He wanted to play with everything,' Mickey said with a frown. 'Anyway, I think I can do something about it. The process can be reversed,' he said with just enough of a pause to give Tails a sinking feeling in his newly burger-filled stomach.

'It can? Is it difficult?'

'Not really,' the monkey said with a lack of conviction. 'I've been reading some vital technical manuals on the subject and I'm pretty sure I know what to do.'

133

'Oh?' said Tails, waiting for more information.

'Yeah. One book on electrical circuits and all that kind of thing. Just to get the details of the machine right. I know the wiring looks a bit dicky, but it'll work handsome, just trust me.'

'What was the other one?' said Tails.

'One of Robotnik's own. *Teach Yourself Brain Control in Ten Easy Lessons*. He got the Mobius Prize for Advanced Eggsperimental Psychology for it, would you blooming believe it?'

'Hmmm.' Tails was very unsure about all this. 'Well, what eggsactly – I mean exactly – are you going to do?' He pointed at the colanders. 'What are they for?'

The monkey was quiet for a minute. 'Have you heard of electronic mind transference?' he said at last.

'I don't think so,' Tails said slowly. 'Is it painful?'

Mickey looked relieved. 'No, it's absolutely not painful at all. Not at all. Right, well that's settled then,' he said hurriedly. 'If you'd just like to park yourself over there, and put the brain transducer on your bonce, we can get this show on the road.'

'Wait a minute!' Tails said equally hurriedly. 'Exactly what are you going to do?'

'Well, it's like this. Robotnik's book has some very interesting things on mind transference. Eggschanging – I mean exchanging; strewth, but that's catching! – the minds of two blokes around.'

'Well, that's no good! Then I'd be a drooling dope like Sonic! Sorry, buddy,' Tails said to his snoozing friend.

'No, no, that's not the idea. What I'm going to do is to link your minds together. Then I'll be able to put your sensible mind into old Sonic. It'll stop him being a drooling loony,' the monkey said uncharitably.

'But won't that just mean that he'll have a mind like mine?'

'No. It'll help him recover his own mind. Look, just trust me, it's a lot easier to do a one-way transfer than an exchange, right? So this'll be a piece of cake, me old mucker.'

'Have you ever done anything like this before?' Tails fretted.

'Don't be ridiculous, it's far too dange– I mean, I've never had any call to, now have I?' Mickey replied reasonably. 'Just give us a hand to carry Sonic over to one of the brain transducers, would you, then all I have to do is to borrow your mind for a minute or two. What could be simpler?'

I don't have much choice, Tails thought sadly. After helping Mickey with the still-sleeping hedgehog, he sat down against the wall and pulled the colander over his head.

'Now, I want you to think really smart thoughts. It's his sense and logic we need to get back,' Mickey said determinedly; he had obviously better start laying the flattery on with a trowel. 'Which should be a pushover, really, since there wasn't too much of that to begin with. You're the smart one, Tails, I know you can do it!'

The fox groaned and tried to think about Really Clever Stuff. For a brief, wonderful second he thought that he could get out of this by getting Porker Lewis, who was definitely the smartest guy around, to take his place. Then he realized that Porker might, at this very second, be turning into a whatsisname, a Senileobite. He shivered and tried to stay calm as the monkey began to flick switches and the hum of powerful electricity filled the room.

'It'll all be over very soon,' said Mickey grimly.

Just before he fell unconscious, it occurred to Tails that if Mickey had got the polarity for the one-way transfer wrong then he'd end up as demented as Sonic! Then his brain went fuzzy all over, just like a jelly-tot after it'd been in your pocket for a few weeks. Just like a . . .

*   *   *

Tails woke to find a very concerned hedgehog shaking him by the shoulders.

'Are you all right, little dude? Oh, that dastardly swine Robotnik!' Sonic lamented. 'Please say you're okay, my foxy pal!'

Tails tried to speak, but he only managed to croak a bit. His throat was very dry and he had to cough to clear it. Then he sneezed loudly and shook a bit. Mickey gave him a paper beaker of cola, which he gulped down thirstily.

'Coochie-coo,' said Tails.

'Mickey, you useless dweeb! You must have exchanged mind states,' Sonic said furiously. 'You've left him a helpless lunatic!'

'I know. Fun isn't it? sniggered Tails. Sonic didn't know whether to be overjoyed or to give Tails a clout around the ears for winding him up so successfully.

'Sorry, Mickey, you are one radically smart dude and a total apology is in order,' Sonic beamed. He surveyed the burned-out wreckage of the Dement Configuration. 'Pity about that, though.'

'Yeah, well, it was a bit on the improvised side,' the monkey said. 'Never mind. It'll all come out in the wash, that's what my old ma used to say.'

'It might have come in useful,' Sonic pondered thoughtfully.

'How so?' Mickey asked.

'Just think what we could have done with Robotnik on the receiving end and a banana at the other,' Sonic chuckled.

'Nah! Waste of a good banana,' Mickey said as he tucked into one of his own. He had just finished it, and unpeeled another, when a bat flew into his hut through the open window and expertly grabbed it and stuffed it into its mouth.

'Hey man!' the monkey started to protest but the bat just

gave him a wink, finished scoffing the fruit and gave him a grin.

'Howdy doody, Mickey,' the bat chuckled. 'I've just come back from Castle Robotnik Stadium. Man, that is one weird playing field. Thought you guys could use a little inside info from the coach,' the bat finished. 'Got any more bananas?' Mickey looked regretful and peeled another one for his hungry visitor, who devoured it.

'Mmmm, that's better,' it said happily. 'Well, Mickey told me about your troubles. And I found a way into the locker room, guys. The big tower right in the middle. Easier than pitching an arm ball. Gather round for a team-talk. Here's how you do it . . .'

Robotnik was beside himself. Well, no, of course he wasn't really. No one can actually be beside themselves or else there would be two of them, but you know what we mean. He was annoyed. Very.

'The Dement Configuration malfunctioned! It should never have been able to allow them to escape the Warp!' he yelled. 'Find the designer and have it melted down for scrap!'

'Er, Master,' Eggor began, but Robotnik interrupted him at once.

'Now! NOW! I want it eggspunged!'

'I'm afraid you designed it yourself, Master,' Eggor said unhappily. There was a moment's silence while Robotnik digested the information, which was more than he'd been able to do with his breakfast eggs. He had a stomach upset from stress. His fat-fingered hands were shaking with the strain.

'Listen, you worthless piece of metal garbage, and listen carefully. In future, if anything like this ever happens again, just find a culprit and melt it down for scrap anyway, right?' Robotnik snarled eggscitedly. 'Don't tell me anything about eggstenuating circumstances, I don't want to hear it. Ha ha ha!'

Eggor allowed himself the tiniest ghost of a smirk. That irritating Spielbot S just might be a plausible culprit if he rigged things right.

'But at least the hedgehog had his brain neutralised,' the robot observed. Robotnik looked slightly cheered up by the thought, but only a little. And not for long.

'The Warps are unpredictable. The process might have been reversed when he entered the Warp,' Robotnik eggslclaimed. 'We cannot eggsclude the possibility.'

Eggor had already anticipated that. 'The computer says there is only a point-one-seven per cent chance of that happening, Master,' he said encouragingly.

Robotnik did seem to be relieved, but then he scowled anyway. 'We can take no chances now. We must complete the Master Eggsperiment and send our creation out to – ha ha ha! – destroy that miserable hedgehog, whether he has his pitifully small brain left or not. Mobius is now ready for my greatest creation. I will unleash – *Frankensonic!*'

Eggor glowed with pleasure. But he had a rival to dispose of first.

'Master, I must check all security points around the castle. Just in case the hedgehog returns yet again. I shall double guard patrols and treble-check the alarm systems. It will take me no more than half an hour.'

'Very good, Eggor,' Robotnik smirked. Now that he'd made his decision, he seemed less eggsplosive, but rather more eggsuberant in a nasty, sadistic, moustache-twirling, wobbly kind of way. He took an egg from the pocket of his white coat and cracked it into his hand, slurping up the thick yolk and runny white. Slobbering eggspressively, he stumped off for the elevator to the great tower, leaving a tiny trail of droplets of egg white dribbling on to the floor as he went.

Eggor keyed in some cursory orders for the guards and

then got down to the real work. If anything went wrong this
time around, there would be a very plausible culprit indeed.
Leaning back after his instructions, he allowed himself a
broad smile, shut down the auxiliary computer systems,
and rubbed his metal hands together with glee.

Now, he thought, first we shall need a replacement
assistant director . . .

Far away, in the Metropolis Zone, Attenbot D took the
call. It would be the greatest outdoors documentary of his
career.

19

RETURN OF THE PSYCHOBUNNY

Sonic and Tails hovered in the air above Castle Robotnik. The fox's twin tails whirled in a blur, making him look like the best helicopter you'd ever seen. Meanwhile, Sonic had propelled himself aloft with a really radically supreme run, leap and spin. To be honest, though, he was not known for his ability to hang in mid-air without some pretty serious help, so right at this moment he was being assisted by a flock of Mickey's bat friends who were delicately gripping his spines and flapping their leathery wings to stay aloft.

'There, you see?' one of the bats was indicating some distant feature. 'Halfway up. Those, my little pitches, are ventilation shafts. It's the one way into this stadium that doesn't involve having to go past those outfield guards at the doors.' It gnawed at a banana and flung the skin through the air, almost hitting the hovering Tails. The fox held out his paws and grabbed it without thinking as it flew towards him.

Looking down, Sonic and Tails could see that several squads of vicious Cluckers and Bomb Bots had both been

positioned to ring the Great Tower at ground level. Since they were among the most dangerous of Robotnik's badniks, it had to be an easier option to enter the castle through a handy ventilation duct than to take all of them on.

'Maximum thanks, little sport-obsessed bat-type dudes. This is radically helpful,' Sonic smiled happily. 'Any time we can, like, return the favour just let me know. But now, I think my bodacious buddy and I are going to go and have a smashing time. Catch you later!'

The hedgehog was released from the bat's grip and shot down towards the metal grille covering the ventilation shafts. As he fell, he twisted into a ball of pure superspinning superhero. He smashed his way through it barely touching the sides, leaving it hanging off its metal hinges, flapping uselessly against the stone wall of the windowless tower. Tails flew right in after him.

'We want to head upwards,' Sonic growled. 'That madman Robotnik is going to be at the top of the tower, of course.'

There was one small problem with that plan. Trying to ascend the ducts, they very nearly ran slap bang into sizzling beams of electricity criss-crossing them. Helpful signs reading 'DANGER: TEN TRILLION MEGAVOLTS!' were hardly necessary to inform them of the hazard. Racing around inside the maze of tunnels, they soon found that every duct leading upwards had the same electrical barrier completely blocking it. It was plain someone had thought of just such a manoeuvre.

'No way up,' Tails lamented. 'Well, it's not surprising really. Anyone would expect him to block such an obvious way upwards past his guards and alarms. Darn that heinous ratfink! We'll have to find a way into the middle floor of the tower and hope we can find an elevator or some stairs going up. There must be some way upwards. I mean, Fatty Robotnik's not going to want to be dropped in by

Egg-o-Matic every time he wants to tinker with his experiment, is he?'

'Good call, little guy. Just one thing: let's not waste time chatting when there's badniks to be a-stomping!' Sonic said impatiently.

Racing around again within the labyrinth of ducts, they soon found large metal grilles which led into the rooms of the middle floor. They all looked very similar: laboratory rooms which were hardly lit at all. The red glow of winking instrument panels and computer consoles flickered eerily in the darkness, but there was no sign of anyone or anything which might get in their way.

'There doesn't seem to be any difference between the different exit points, Sonic,' Tails said. 'Can't hear much either, apart from the odd click or bleep here and there. There don't seem to be any badniks clanking about, that's one good thing. Which one do you think we should –'

'The nearest one,' Sonic laughed as he spun full-pelt into the grille ahead of him and sent it flying into the room with a loud clatter.

'We could just have unscrewed and dismantled it; it would have been quieter,' Tails protested, but he knew Sonic too well to argue the point. When the bodacious hedgehog gets whizzing, the finer points of subtlety and the need for stealth are totally lost on him.

Sonic flicked on a light switch he had found by feeling his way around the walls. The room just seemed to be full of machinery, and there was nothing to show what the peculiar devices did. That was cool: after his exploits in the boiler room, Sonic wasn't in any great hurry to find out. He wanted to get out and get upwards, to find Robotnik and put a stop to his heinous schemes. He let Tails open the door rather than smashing it down, much as he eagerly wanted to.

Outside the room, all appeared quiet. The two heroes

stepped into the passage beyond. A low buzzing drone, sounding faint in the distance, began to get louder.

Sonic turned to his foxy pal. 'Just don't say "Can you hear something?", little buddy, because I most assuredly can,' he warned. 'Could be Buzzers, could be worse. Let's get moving before they get here.'

Looking around for elevators or staircases as they headed on along the passage, and finding none, the two of them were very aware that the droning sound was getting louder and louder. And *louder*. And LOUDER.

'We're going to have to do some badnik-smashing,' Sonic smirked. 'What a shame!'

'Oh dear, how sad, never mind!' grinned back Tails.

Sonic began to work himself up into a spin. He was expected Buzzers, or some kind of badnik. He wasn't expecting a masked rabbit with a chainsaw.

'What?' Sonic blurted in surprise when the familiar shape rounded the corner in the passage and strode confidently towards them. 'Hey you, Bugs Brainless, you bought it in that pit. Slice-and-dice time for psychobunnies! We saw it ourselves!'

'Huh,' the rabbit snarled dismissively. 'Don't you know Jase never dies? It's always Friday and there's always a sequel, deadhog. Except for you!' With that, he rushed forward to attack, chainsaw at the ready. Sonic ducked and spun as only he knew how.

Tails was right in the line of fire. Trying to dodge aside, he could see the rabbit veering right for him, swinging the chainsaw in a wide arc, filling the passage. Those of a nervous disposition, and all those for whom the sight of a dismembered sidekick might be distressing, are advised not to watch at this point. Sorry, people, but it looked like the cute little fellow was on a one-way trip to Foxslice City.

Tails took a step to the left. The chainsaw-wielding

bunny from hell did the same. Tails jumped back to the right, but the rabbit matched his movements exactly. There was no escape.

Crikey! thought Tails desperately, I'm only moments away from kissing my arms and legs good-bye and I appear to be dancing The Timewarp with a power-tool-packing carrot cruncher. Is there no way out? Is this really the end of poor little me? Is there . . . Hey! Hold up a minute; what's this in my pocket?

'Aha!' he cried aloud, and with that Tails played his master stroke. With a smooth action perfected over many happy evenings tossing about his favourite yellow frisbee, he flung the banana skin he'd inadvertently stuck in his pocket when the bat had heaved it his way. It landed right beneath the advancing Jase's feet.

The rabbit went head over heels and his chainsaw flew across the floor, bouncing and whining as it chewed its way through carpet and lino tiles. It went right on bouncing harmlessly along the passage and came to rest, stalling, against the wall. Sonic spun down and biffed the rabbit hard on the back of his head. Jase crumpled up in a heap on the floor and lay still.

'Yikes! That was close. We'd better get moving before he wakes up,' Tails said anxiously.

Clanking sounds came from the same direction which Jase had appeared from. Sonic readied himself for an instant change of gear all the way up to Attack Mode.

'Look, if we leave him here he may not raise an alarm. He might just have tripped up and had an accident, for all a dumb bunch of robots will know,' Tails pleaded. 'I mean, look at that chainsaw; talk about dangerous; I bet he's always doing himself a mischief with it. We don't want to waste energy here. There'll be enough time for smashing when we get to the top, remember?'

'Why do you always spoil my fun?' Sonic grumbled, but

he knew that Tails was right. 'Okay dude, you're talking sense . . .' .

Tails beamed.

'Just this once,' Sonic finished. Tails stuck out his tongue at him. 'Let's move on out. We've still got a long way to go!'

They raced along the corridor, but screeched to a halt as they passed a door marked 'E.LEVATOR'. Unfortunately, they were in such a hurry they clean failed to notice that crucial full stop.

'In here!' Tails said, pushing the door open and jumping in. Sonic leapt into the darkness behind him and shut the door behind him to keep the oncoming robots at bay. It was very dark in the elevator.

Now, where are those flipping buttons, Sonic thought, stretching out his hands and feeling around the metal walls. He pressed the first one he found. The lights came on at once.

There was a helpful sign hanging on one wall of the room. It read 'PROTOTYPE DEVELOPMENT LABORA-TORY'. Hanging up on pegs on the wall were white lab coats, each bearing a badge with the name 'Dr Ernest Levator, Assistant to Professor Robotnik' sewn on to them.

'Oh come on, Sonic. It was an easy mistake to make,' Tails said apologetically. Robots were clanking down the passage outside. It clearly wasn't safe to leave just yet, not without raising the alarm anyway, and that was what they were really worried about.

'What is this place?' Sonic asked, prodding at the metal cages and electronic machinery which littered the room. He prodded one thing too many, as usual.

There was a loud ringing sound of metal hitting the hard laboratory floor. At once, the door behind them clicked shut and electronically locked itself. One of the computer screens leaped into life, bearing the message 'SPECIMEN

FREED IN PDL! SECURITY RESPONSE ACTIVATION!'.
At the same moment, a loud *Wooo-wooo*ing sound, a
wailing electronic alarm, started to scream its baleful tone
throughout the room.

'Oh, Sonic, what have you done?' Tails groaned as he
held his hands over his ears. Looking at the hedgehog, he
suddenly saw what had emerged from the cage Sonic had
inadvertently opened. His jaw dropped. Sonic saw the look
on his face and whirled around.

It was a spider. Well, okay, yes it was, but what a spider!
It was two metres wide and it had legs longer than the
fashion models on the pop-video channels, and far more
hairy to boot. Glowing red eyes the colour of cola cans
glared at the intruders. It slowly opened its jaws to reveal
huge ripping teeth and poisonous drool dripped from its
twitching mouth, as if to say 'Have a look at these, you
schmucks; big, aren't they?'. This was one spider no one
was going to flush down the plug-hole. It raised itself up on
four of its massive legs and began to move towards Sonic
and Tails.

'Eeek! Poison! It's a mutant!' Tails yelped. As the thing
got closer, he could see that it wasn't just a normal gigantic,
two-metre mutant spider either (if you know what we
mean). It seemed to have been stitched together from
various bits of different gigantic, two-metre mutant spiders.
Its legs were each a different colour to the rest of its body,
and its head was far too large for its bulbous body. It was
very scary and smelled extremely unpleasant.

Sonic and Tails ran around in panic, trying to keep long
work benches and racks of cages between them and the
lumbering spider. It spat a gob of acid poison at them which
they managed to duck, but when the viscous gunge hit the
far wall it peeled off the paint and left a sizzling brown stain
that totally clashed with the rest of the decor.

'Oh, gross,' Tails groaned. 'Robotnik's breeding

mutants and monsters! And I just bet it's not to use them in the decorating business as handy mobile paint strippers.'

'Of course he is,' Sonic growled. 'Prototype Development Laboratory, right? A prototype for his monsters. What he wants to turn us into. This is totally heinous! And look, it's even in his wretched movie!'

Tails dared to look up as another gobbet of super spider spit sped just over his head. The ever-present movie cameras were mounted at the top of the walls, whirring around to track their every move. Just then the laboratory door opened, and metal clanking came from outside as something shiny and metallic rushed in. They were trapped, caught between mutants and badniks!

Robotnik stared in disbelief at the camera monitors as the Bomb Bot exploded in the centre of the Prototype Development Laboratory and blew the mutant spider to pieces. It also managed to destroy a vast amount of valuable equipment and most of the Crawlers the crazed doctor had sent in to kill of Sonic and Tails. Wobbling with pent-up volcanic fury, he could do nothing more than watch the hated hedgehog and his annoying twin-tailed friend skip over the wreckage and leave the disaster zone with nothing so much as a scratch. When they hit the corridor outside, he saw a close-up of Sonic's smirking face as he bounced up at the cameras tracking him, and then the monitor screens went blank. Every monitoring camera was swiftly destroyed by the angry hedgehog and fox.

'Eggor! What has happened? This is ineggsplicable! Find out who is responsible!'

Smirking just out of sight of his master, Eggor rattled one metal hand on the keyboard as he feigned some fast computer analysing. 'Ah, I think I have found the problem, Master,' he said smoothly after a few moments of apparent investigation.

'Well? What is it? No eggscuses!'

'Apparently, Master, Spielbot made the movie *Attack of the Killer Mutant Spiders from the Plant Zorg* in the laboratory a year or so ago.'

'Yes, and?' Robotnik said suspiciously.

'The Bombot was a security device planted to make sure the spider didn't escape in the original movie. It had not been correctly re-programmed since that film was made.'

'Then that is your fault! You are responsible for security!' Robotnik screamed with his best 'you are about to hit melt-down' eggspression on his face.

'Um, no, I hate to contradict you, Master, but that is not so. I wasn't here when the film was made,' Eggor said calmly. 'There was also a specific priority over-ride in my instructions from yourself, master, not to deal with security in this laboratory.' He offered him a handy printout from the computer to prove his point. Robotnik studied it and calmed down a little.

'Very well. You are eggsonerated, Eggor. So, who was responsible for the security there?'

'Spielbot S, master. Because of the film-making. He was given overall control of all aspects of the scene, including security.'

'Then have him found and melted down for scrap!' Robotnik screamed. 'Ha ha ha!'

They were the words Eggor had wanted to hear for days, and in the end they had proved so simple to obtain. Now the *Castle Robotnik* movie would be his, all his, and he would get the true star's role he deserved. His metal chest swelled with pride.

'I don't know how we got out of that,' Tails chuckled as they searched for an elevator to the top of the tower and Robotnik's master laboratory.

'Malfunctioning badnik, I expect,' Sonic said. 'Robotnik

does make mistakes, you know. And hey, here come some more of them!' The clanking of robots was clearly audible in the distance. 'Let's get bouncing!'

'Wait,' Tails sighed. 'We agreed that we needed to conserve our energies for Robotnik himself, right?' He pulled Sonic into a small clean-up room with a glass panel set in the door, and with their noses pressed against the window they waited to see what nasties were heading their way now.

The robots looked very sinister. There were modified Grabbers and even two multi-gun Cluckers, and a towering Slicer that looked very menacing indeed. They were black-lacquered and looked for all the world as if they were wearing black top hats and long frock coats with tails at the back (but not foxy tails, if you know what we mean). The Cluckers had the words 'MELT-DOWN SQUAD' painted on their backs in old-fashioned joined-up letters. The sinister group continued past Sonic and Tails's hiding place and thankfully clanked off down the corridor into the distance.

Tails and Sonic emerged slowly, peering carefully around the door until they were sure that there were no more badniks in the offing. Tails noticed something lying on the floor, bent down and picked up a glossy embossed card that one of the robots appeared to have dropped along the way.

'Hmmmm. "Dr Ivo Robotnik & Associates, Funeral Directors." What can it mean?'

20

TOTAL MELT-DOWN

Spielbot S crossed from the Tower of Power after another interview, this time for the RBC; that's the Robotnik Broadcasting Corporation, one of Robotnik's string of TV stations. It's strange; Robotnik owned masses of them, all pumping out entertainment for his robot minions around Mobius around the clock, but every programme on every single one of them was rubbish. Sounds familiar?

He was happy, because he'd been interviewed by a robot with a truly exceptional Grovelling Program installed into it and it had asked really dead-brain questions that he'd been able to answer while at the same time looking great and talking platitudes as usual. As he glided along happily, his attention was caught by a group of sinister black robots pouring out of the Great Tower, and they seemed to be heading toward him. Funny, he thought, I don't remember hiring them for the movie.

'Are you Spielbot, designation S?' snarled the leader of the group. It was an exceptionally large Slicer and it looked extremely nasty. Spielbot got a sinking feeling deep in his

central circuit boards as he began to suspect something awful was just about to happen.

'Er, no. He's still in the Tower of Power, in the hospitality room,' he replied.

'Are you sure? You look an awful lot like the holographic image I have installed in my seek-and-destroy program,' the Slicer said in a deathly tone of voice.

Spielbot almost panicked but managed to keep an even voice. 'That's because I'm his assistant and he likes his assistants to look like him,' he said, keeping his voice as flat as possible to sound plausible.

'Hmmm. Maybe I should melt you down anyway. Just in case,' the Slicer said threatingly.

'Oh no, Dr Robotnik wouldn't like that at all. If you melt me down as well as Spielbot then his great movie won't get finished on time, and then Dr Robotnik won't be able to win the Mobius Prize for Film Production and Direction. Then he'll get eggstremely angry and he will blame you, and that wouldn't do at all, would it? You'd have to melt yourself down.'

The Slicer had one of those 'I'm not sure about how it has happened, but you've got off the hook' expressions on its face. 'Very well,' it growled and headed off to the Tower of Power with its strike team.

Spielbot hurried for the master laboratory as fast as his tracks could carry him to find out what on Mobius was going on. How could Robotnik want him melted down for scrap when he had all but completed his master's magnum opus? He had to find out. There had to be some mistake somewhere.

Just as Eggor was about to leave the master laboratory for the Great Tower, Robotnik reappeared in the doorway.

'Eggor, one last thing,' the white-coated lunatic growled. 'Have – ha ha ha! – Spielbot's film crew melted down for scrap as well.'

'What, master?' Eggor was staggered; this wasn't part of the plan at all. 'But, master, then the movie will never be made!'

'I've changed my mind,' Robotnik said. 'We can't trust those robots. They may be spies or terrorists. Remember that dratted Bomb Bot. Spielbot's robots cannot be trusted! They must be eggspunged! Ha ha ha!'

'But it was just that its instructions weren't repro-grammed correctly. It was a simple computer error,' Eggor argued.

'Don't you dare argue with me!' Robotnik yelled. 'Have those robots melted down NOW – or else! No eggscuses! Issue the orders now, Eggor, then join me atop the tower.' He stomped off.

Eggor was beside himself. Now he would never have his starring role in the movie! He knew, or he thought he knew, that his Master might change his mind later and then it would be too late if the film crew had already been eggster-minated. Unless, unless . . . he recalled the one film unit left to him!

He keyed in his last set of orders in double-quick time and left for the top of the Great Tower. Unfortunately, in his haste to join his master, he made the dreadful mistake of not shutting down the central computer access. Why are we pointing out this apparently insignificant detail? Just wait and see.

'There must be an elevator around here somewhere,' Tails said fretfully. 'How else can smelly old Robotnik get to the top of the tower without one?'

They were getting just a little tired and peeved with all this dashing around. They'd jogged round almost the entire middle floor of the tower, and couldn't find an elevator anywhere. Heck, they hadn't come across so much as a step-ladder. They had come across two patrolling groups

of Crawltons, but our heroes had disposed of those easily enough.

Now their plentiful supplies of peanut-butter-and-jelly sarnies that Mickey had thoughtfully supplied were all scoffed and they didn't have much in the way of nuts or crisps left to fuel Sonic's superfast metabolism.

'At last!' Sonic grumbled. 'Look.' He pointed to the end of the corridor. A pair of sliding metal doors stood innocently there, not really doing all that much, in the manner of doors. 'That's got to be it.'

The indicator panel above the door winked on, with a red electronic arrow pointing upwards suddenly flashing at them.

'Yikes! Something's on the way, let's hide. At least until we see what it is,' Tails suggested.

Despite his impatience, which was now so peeved he feared it would burst out of his body, Sonic agreed with his furry pal. His hero-type energy needed to be preserved for the final confrontation with Robotnik. They hid along a side-passage as the sound of metal clanking approached from the distance.

The single robot passed by them without a glance, headed for Robotnik's computer laboratory. They ducked out behind it and raced into the elevator just as the Spielbot keyed in his security code and made for the computer console in the computer laboratory.

Inside the elevator, Sonic pressed the button marked with an upwards-pointing arrow.

Back in the computer laboratory, Spielbot S desperately started beavering away in an attempt to find out why an order had been given to have him melted down for scrap.

Spielbot wasn't experienced in using computer-data systems. He didn't know Robotnik's access codes and, worst of all, he didn't know that Robotnik hadn't yet filed any data on his upcoming eggstermination. Furiously, Spielbot scanned what little data he had managed to get access to.

'Curses! Curses!' Spielbot screamed, jumping up and down and smashing a metal fist into the console. He hit something vital. The equipment sparked and the screens went black for a couple of seconds. A power unit in the corner of the room exploded and blew sheets of metal panelling into the room, which in turn shattered another group of computer units right by it. By the time the sparking and explosions had stopped, the entire building had been plunged into pitch darkness.

'What's happened?' Tails squeaked. The lights in the elevator had all gone out and the thing ground to a halt in the middle of the elevator shaft. 'Oh no! Robotnik must have seen us in here and he's stopped the elevator! We're caught like rats in a trap!'

'Stop squeaking, little dude; we're not rats. I'm a way-cool hedgehog and you're his cute fox sidekick, and we're both superdudes, stars of stage, screen and MegaDrive,' Sonic said sternly. Winding himself up for a vertical leap, he hurled himself at the top of the elevator, hoping to burst the metal door set there off its hinges. All he got for his pains was a nasty (not to mention clashing) pink bump on his head and the beginnings of an unpleasant headache.

'This is going to take longer than I thought,' he snarled, 'but we're going to get there, buddy, don't you worry.'

'What has happened? Eggor?' Robotnik screamed with rage in the darkness.

'Switching to emergency back-up,' came the reassuring voice of his assistant from just below a pair of dim yellow circles. It didn't calm Robotnik's frayed nerves.

'We must eggspedite the completion of my – ha ha ha! –

marvellous eggsperiment! That wretched hedgehog is in the building and now we will not be able to track him with cameras! Quickly, Eggor!'

Faint, flickering electrical light re-lit the ghastly scene atop the tower. Robotnik looked especially sinister in the shadows which still haunted the nooks and crannies of the tower.

'The emergency back-up systems are also damaged, Master. I estimate that even this meagre power will only hold for twelve-point-seven-two minutes,' the robot reported sadly. 'I estimate the problem to be an eggsplosion in the computer laboratory. Repair system monitors estimate that completion time for repairing all of the damage will be twenty-three-point-five-five hours.'

'What? That dastardly hedgehog! I will have him eggspunged if it's the last thing I ever do!' yelled Robotnik, almost purple with fury.

'The one functioning sensor in the laboratory shows that there was no life form there when the eggsplosion occurred,' Eggor said. 'However, Spielbot S is in the laboratory now.'

'What?' Eggor thought that Robotnik was actually going to eggsplode himself. 'But I gave orders for him to be melted down!'

'The Melt-Down Squad was despatched as you ordered, master,' Eggor replied unhappily. 'But there is no doubt that the Spielbot in question caused the explosion.' Actually, Eggor was, well, eggstrapolating a bit, but he got away with it.

'Melt him down! Melt everything down!' Robotnik had gone through fury and rage, and his personal looneyometer was now hovering somewhere near the middle of total manic dementia. 'We can never finish this eggsperiment without more power! I must have more power! Ha ha haaaa!!!'

'Master, Master!' Eggor yelled above the screams of his deranged master, 'I know how the eggsperiment can be completed.'

'We cannot wait a whole day for power to be returned! Ha ha haaaaa!'

'No, twenty-three-point-five-five hours,' Eggor said pedantically. 'However, I have A Plan. The eggsperiment can be completed very swiftly, Master. For look, I have just accessed the weather reports.'

'The weather report? At a time like this you worry about the weather? Melt yourself down for scrap this instant!' Robotnik screamed. His moustaches trembled with frustration and he almost skipped on the spot, he was wobbling so much. Let's face it, he was making a real eggshibition of himself.

'Wait, master. This is my plan . . .'

Robotnik listened. As Eggor eggsplained, he began to calm down just a little. By the time the robot had finished, he even allowed himself a small smile.

'I have already ordered a squadron of Egg-o-Matics to transport the eggsperiment across,' Eggor smirked.

'Good robot! Ha ha ha! Good, good robot! Eggor, I knew that recreating you was one of my best moments of unique genius!'

'Thank you, Master.' Eggor felt as if the world had just fallen at his feet.

'Why didn't we bring a spanner?' groaned Tails. 'We could have got those super-tough titanium-steel plate bolts off two shakes of a two-tailed fox's tails.'

'Because we're not plumbers,' Sonic growled. 'We're working for the other side, the good guys; remember?' The hedgehog wrenched another bolt from the ceiling with a mighty pull. He was getting fatigued, frustrated and very bored trying to disassemble the escape hatch atop the elevator.

'It seems very stupid to me to have an escape hatch and then make it virtually impossible to escape from it,' he snarled. Looking down, he saw a fox trying hard not to look at him. He was suspicious immediately.

'What is it?' he demanded. The fox continued staring at the opposite wall of the elevator.

Sonic looked too. There was a small metal box with a glass front mounted on the wall, and above it was a small hammer. A sign fixed over the box read 'IN CASE OF EMERGENCY BREAK THE GLASS'.

Inside the box was a spanner.

One smashed box later, and a furious few seconds of crazed spanner-waggling after that, Sonic and Tails successfully clambered on top of the elevator cubicle and stared up at the chains and levers above them.

'Let's get climbing, dude. I can see the end of the book coming up fast and we've still got a ton of hero stuff to fit in,' Sonic said grimly.

'Well done, luvs,' said the directing robot as the rats finally finished devouring the biggest baconburger in the history of Mobius. 'A simply lovely take. Super, absolutely super.' It spoke with all the sincerity of a politician on the telly: i.e., None At All.

'Unfortunately, luvs, we have another project to work on now. We've just had fresh orders. We're going to be filming the climactic scenes of a guaranteed Eggscar-winning movie,' it said with pride. It was thinking of an Eggscar for itself. It realised its mistake immediately, and wished that it had had a Discretion Circuit installed.

'An Eggscar winner?' Capone growled softly. 'Well, now, that's interesting, isn't it boys?'

The rats snarled agreement a bit uncertainly. Most of them didn't even know what an Eggscar was.

'Thug like Eggscars,' the barbarian intoned. He was a bit

sore after wrestling a twenty-metre-tall pig to the ground, and he didn't know anything about art, but he sure knew what he liked.

'I think we oughta be in this movie, don't you?' Capone snarled. Heads nodded all around him.

'But, luvvies, darlings, please be reasonable. There aren't any parts in it for you,' the robot pleaded.

'Get the screenwriter to write some,' Drizzle yelled, 'or else he gets a dose of the Ebon Staff of Peaminster the Magnificent!'

'Yeah,' Capone agreed, since he was holding it. 'So what's this wonderful movie called anyway?'

'Well, um, I can reveal to you at this time that it's called *Castle Robotnik*. It's a monster movie,' the robot said helplessly.

'Monsters! Will there be any Foul Dragons to slay?' asked Sir Norbert.

'Not as such,' the robot said. 'There's something much bigger, actually.'

'Bigger than a Mighty Dragon? It's not a Twenty-Metre Chaos Death Dino-pig, is it?' asked Sir Norbert suspiciously.

'Definitely not. But it's a Secret,' the robot said pompously.

'You better tell me, tough guy, or else you get can get staffed,' said Capone, pointing the Ebon Staff squarely at him. The robot flinched metallically.

'But, luvvie, I don't know what it is. That's why it's a Secret,' it pleaded.

'We are wasting time on our epic quest!' Sir Norbert shouted. 'We must begone to dire, dark, doom-filled Castle· Robotnik and –'

'– kill Gazza the Dark Lord again, I suppose,' came a sarcastic female voice.

'– kill Gazza the Dark Lord! No, of course not,' the

paladin babbled confusedly. 'We must slay the dire, dark, doom-filled secret of dire, damp, dark –'

'Yes, we get the idea, you chinless dweeb,' Capone growled at him. 'Now let's get moving. It's beginning to get dark, there's a storm on the way, and it's a fair hike to that Scrap Brain Zone.'

'Do we have the infra-red night-time cameras for filming the secretive little animals?' Attenbot D was asking his robotic technician.

'Check,' the robot said.

'And we have sent out the field crew to make those clever hiding places from where we can film them without disturbing them?'

'Check,' the technician said again.

'We have the jeeps and trucks to transport everything?'

'Check,' the technician said automatically.

'How are we going to get paid?'

'Cheque,' the technician said again.

'Right then. Let's go shoot some animals.'

21

ROBOTNIK EGGSCAPES!

'We can leap across from here,' Sonic panted to Tails as they hung precariously at the top of the elevator chains. They were fifteen metres above the elevator now. It seemed an awfully long drop.

The fox twirled his tails into action and zipped over to the ledge by the elevator doors to the top floor. 'How are we going to open them?' he said.

'This, little dude, is a time for deeds of super-bodacious heroism!' Sonic cried. Whipping himself up into a Super-Spin from a standing start – and let us tell you, that isn't easy even for a hero of the stature of our beloved Sonic, so don't try this at home, kids – he smashed into the doors. For a horrible split-second it looked as if they would just get dented a little and a tiny, insignificant little hedgehog was going to bounce off them and hit the elevator roof far, far below. Then they swished open, Sonic hanging on to one of them and scrabbling on the floor beyond in an instant.

'We're in,' he gasped. 'Cowabunga, but that was a radi-cally close call. Now let's find that eggy ratfink Robotnik

and put a stop to what's he doing up here once and for all.'

The top floor of the castle was more like a dungeon. Cold stone walls held the familiar torches, but they weren't burning and there was very little light by which to see.

'Huh, just bogus imitations,' Sonic sniffed disdainfully as he examined one of the torches. 'It's actually lit with an electric light bulb. How naff can you get?'

'That means the power isn't turned on up here either,' Tails reasoned. 'That's interesting. There must have been an electrical breakdown or something.'

Sonic's eyes gleamed. 'And that'll mean that Robotnik's alarms and traps may not be working properly! Hey, is this Lucky Day City or what? Let's find him fast!'

He sped off along the passages, kicking open doors, ignoring the network of laboratories that didn't have a Robotnik in them. At last, after a great deal of door kicking, neck craning and subsequent corridor zooming, they found the master laboratory.

Robotnik was standing on the far side of the room, just about to clamber into an Egg-o-Matic from a hatch that had opened in the wall. Outside and beyond him, rain was beginning to lash down and thunder rolled in the skies. Mobius was having another of its really bad nights. Its resident owls were meeting urgently to consider a proposed suicide pact.

'You are too late, you wretched hedgehog! Ha ha ha! Soon my master creation will be set loose upon Mobius and destroy you and your insufferable animal friends! Ha-ha-ha haa!' Robotnik wriggled with glee. It was a truly disgusting sight, like nothing so much as seventeen ferrets fighting inside a bean-bag.

'Not so fast, you bloated over-brained badnik!' Sonic yelled at him, but his flying and spinning were too late. Robotnik squeezed himself into his flying ship and sped into the night.

'Where's he going?' Tails yelled. 'Keep an eye on him!'

It was dark and pouring with rain, but Sonic kept looking at the Egg-o-Matic. Unfortunately, it flew behind the Tower of Power and was lost to sight.

'Heinous curses! He's got away,' Sonic growled. 'Well, at least we might be able to find out what he's been doing here.'

'Yes, we need to know how to help poor old Porker,' Tails pointed out.

They began a quick look round in the fading light. The most obvious thing in the huge workshop was a twenty-metre-long vast wooden slab. Robotnik must have felled half a rain-forest to make it, which is just the kind of horrid thing that odious bloated toad would do. Huge leather straps were bolted to it, with enormous buckles to secure them, as if to tie down something ginormous beyond the ordinary conception of your average hero-type dudes.

'I don't believe that,' Tails said. 'What on Mobius can he have that's that flipping big? And what's more, where is it now?'

Sonic, meanwhile, was looking disbelievingly up at a twenty-metre-high hatch in the wall just by the place Robotnik had escaped from.

'I think it got out through there,' he said. 'It must have needed a dozen Egg-o-Matics to get it out.'

'Unless it can fly,' Tails said.

'I don't, like, even want to *consider* that possibility,' Sonic said dryly.

They searched the place as thoroughly as they could, but they found virtually nothing. All they did turn up were some doodles on scraps of papers with the heading 'Computer Laboratory' at the top of them. They couldn't make any sense out of them.

'Wait a minute. The computer laboratory is on the middle floor,' Tails said. 'That robot we passed went into it. We

could check there. It's got to be our best chance.'

'That means climbing back down into the elevator.'

'Yes, I suppose so.'

'And then undoing the bolts in the door in the floor.'

'Well, at least we've got a spanner now.'

'And then climbing down to get back to the middle floor.'

'Yes, there's that too.'

'And smashing open the doors there. It might not be so easy a second time.'

'Yeah, okay, clever clogs. But do you have a better idea?'

'Sure,' Sonic sniggered. 'I'm standing on a trapdoor. Bet you there's a secret set of steps leading down to the middle floor beneath it.'

Spielbot S was panicking. At any moment he was expecting a group of black robots to turn up and arrange an immediate funeral for him. The power had almost completely failed now, and he still hadn't find out anything about his predicament. He was so intent on scrabbling at the computer console that he didn't hear the softly approaching footstep sounds until it was too late.

'Don't move. There's a loaded spanner at your back and I'm not afraid to use it. One false move and you're going to be dismantled,' came a distinctly hedgehoggy voice.

'All right. Please don't do that. I've got a wifedroid and three babybots to support,' the robot pleaded.

'You should have thought about them before you got yourself into this sorry mess. What are you doing?'

'I'm trying to find out why Dr Robotnik, world-famous super-genius and brilliant movie producer –'

There was a very menacing growl from directly behind him. Spielbot changed his speech very hastily.

'– has ordered me to be melted down for scrap.'

'Oh, really?' said Tails, and then he had a brainwave.

'Oh, really! Well, what with the power failure here, you can't actually be melted down right now. We were sent to dismantle you instead. However, in the interests of discovering what caused the power failure and dealing with it, we might spare you if you provide us some important information.'

Sonic looked at his buddy with something approaching admiration. He was impressed.

'What do you want to know?' Spielbot said. The thought of his imminent dismantling made him scared, and he couldn't concentrate properly.

'Well, first we need to know about the *Castle Robotnik* movie so that we can help repair the damage,' Tails said. It wasn't an enormously plausible argument, but Spielbot was too fearful to think straight.

Spielbot began telling them everything they wanted to know, and a lot more besides. By the time he'd finished, if anyone had asked them to fill in a detailed questionnaire on their current mental state, Sonic and Tails could only have ticked the box marked 'Totally gobsmacked'.

'My plate mail is going to rust in this,' Sir Norbert complained as they trudged through the undergrowth. 'Not to mention my weapon.'

'That's never been anything to write home about,' Bimbette said dryly. For a hastily constructed actor-droid she sure had some bottle. 'I wouldn't worry about it, Nobby.'

A gleam of metal could suddenly be seen lurking in the undergrowth as a flash of lightning illuminate the night-time sky. A detachment of rats sneaked into the shrubs and ferns to surround whatever it was. The sound of rodent snarls and the whip of ropes being flung around metal told everyone they'd caught something.

'Help me,' pleaded the small robot they'd captured. It

resembled one of Robotnik's Caterkillers, but its eyes were now glowing a dull red.

'A spy!' Capone snarled. 'Let's do some improvised junking work, guys.'

'No! Please! I'm just a helpless little cambot,' the robot whined. 'With infra-red lenses for night-time work. Please don't do anything nasty to me, Mr Rat, sir.'

'A cambot?' the directing robot said suspiciously. 'What are you doing here?'

'Making a wildlife documentary,' the cambot said.

'Oh yeah?' snarled the directing robot. 'Who for?'

'Attenbot D, the infinitely famous documentary maker and winner of the All-Mobius All-Round Darn Nice Droid Award three years running,' the cambot said proudly.

'Never heard of him!' spat Capone.

'This is an outrage!' the director said furiously. 'He's trying to steal my movie, is he? We'll soon see about that. Where's his hide-out then?'

'Just over there,' the cambot indicated with a flick of its round head. 'See that tree that looks like a tree? It's actually a carefully constructed production complex with an array of sound recording devices, infra-red cameras and –'

'Yes, I can imagine,' the director said. It stomped off to the tree and hammered on it. A metal head poked out and the sound of a distant commentary could be heard coming from inside.

'. . . and here we see the feral Mobius rat, *Rattus rattus Robotnikus*, in a most unusual environment. These scavengers are most active in the night-time hours –'

'Scavengers?' Capone yelled furiously. 'Who is this soon-to-be-an-ex-jerk?'

'That's Mr Attenbot,' the cambot said proudly. 'Isn't he good?'

'– and they are noted for their frequent disposition to mindless violence,' the Attenbot continued. He wasn't in the hut, himself, but his commentary was being relayed through from a distant location.

'You're stealing my movie,' the director said to the metal head that had poked itself out of the door to the hideout.

'Why don't you just run off and rust somewhere, little droid?' said the other robot contemptuously. 'I've got an award-winning documentary to finish.'

The director pulled its head off.

Capone gave it a whole new look of respect. 'Now, that's the way to go,' he yelled. 'Wipe-out time, boys. Trash everything!'

A rodent crowd noted for its frequent predisposition to mindless violence set about the handful of robots left in the film-making hide-out. After only a few seconds, there was nothing left intact, bar the one monitor showing the Attenbot, and Sir Norbert put his sword through that. Obviously, since the weapon was made of metal, and so was the twerp on the other end of it, he got electrocuted, but then he wasn't a terribly intelligent android at the best of times.

22

FRANKENSONIC LIVES!

'So he's building a twenty-metre-tall, giant killer hedgehog that looks just like an XL version of me?' Sonic enquired incredulously.

'Look, I've told you three times already. It was going to be the epic scene at the end of the movie. It was going to clamber to its enormous feet and squash, er, certain intruders,' Spielbot said. By now, he'd figured out that he'd dug a seriously deep hole for himself. It was only after he'd finished blabbing out everything he knew that he had realized that Sonic and Tails were the ones standing behind him. By then, of course, it was too late.

'Oh yeah, those gorillas, right?' Tails asked, remembering the radio broadcast from much earlier in the plot.

Spielbot was completely confused now.

'Well, it doesn't matter now. All we need to know is, where is Robotnik now that he's fled the lab at the top of the tower? Tell us that and you can go back to your babybots,' Sonic offered.

'That's the problem. I don't know,' the Spielbot pleaded.

'Honestly, I don't. Ow! Get that spanner off my steel-dermal plating. It frightens me.'

'Talk or else!' Tails tried one last time.

'I don't know!!!'

'He doesn't know,' Sonic said sadly.

'How many times do I have to tell you that?' the robot pleaded.

His speech was interrupted by an enormous thunder-clap which exploded in the air directly over the castle. Tails wanted to put his paws over his ears, but he held the spanner to Spielbot's back for dear life. Just at that moment, as if the lightning had been intended for him, a brilliant idea came into his mind.

'Sonic! I know where he's gone!' he said excitedly. 'Think about it. He needs electrical power to complete animating this heinous thing, right?'

'Right,' Sonic said, waiting for Tails to get to the blooming point, as per usual.

'There isn't any left here, right?'

'Right again. So?'

'Come with me,' Tails said.

'If you move, you're an ex-robot,' Sonic snarled to the Spielbot. The cowardly droid sat straight upright in his chair and didn't move his metal body one centimetre.

'Let's take a look. Through this hatch Spielbot showed us.' Tails and Sonic tugged furiously at the sealed doors. Finally, they prised them a few centimetres apart.

'There!' Tails said triumphantly.

Sonic looked across at the Tower of Power. Atop it, the radio antenna glowed white as a bolt of lightning struck it from the storm-filled skies.

'Of course,' the hedgehog breathed, punching one tightly clenched fist into the other hand, just like he'd seen them do in the movies. 'I saw the Egg-o-Matic disappear on the far side of it. There must be another of these secret

hatches over there, and he flew into it. But how are we going to get across? This tower is surrounded by Cluckers and worse.'

'We'll have to fly. We can do it,' Tails said.

'You realise that that means getting back into the elevator shaft.'

'Yes, that's true.'

'And climbing back up into the elevator.'

'I know.'

'Then climbing up the chains to the top floor again.'

'Dreadful, isn't it? Wait a minute, haven't we had a conversation like this before?'

'Yes, you silly fox,' Sonic shrugged, aiming a friendly swipe just over his head. 'You're forgetting that we found those secret steps, right? Dimbo!'

Tails clapped his paws to his head. He'd been so bound up in his own idea, and thinking about what they could do when they reached the Tower of Power, that he'd entirely forgotten about the steps.

'Let's get moving. And you, don't you move or else –'

Sonic looked around angrily. While he and Tails had been standing looking out into the night, that Spielbot had sneaked away.

'He may be raising the alarm!' Tails yelled. 'There's no time to lose!'

They sped up the stairs, across the top of the tower, and leapt out into the stormy night. It was do-or-die time for Mobius's greatest (not to mention only) super-dudes!

'Say, you're not the pathetic, chinless, metal dweeb-brain I thought you were,' Capone said. 'I like your style. Pulling the heads off things – that's cool.'

'It was nothing,' the directing robot said modestly.

'I don't even know your name,' Capone commented as

they reached the margins of Scrap Brain Zone. 'What's your handle?'

'My friends call me Unit 7264D,' the robot said confidentially.

'Huh,' Capone said. 'That's no kind of a name. Look, dude, you need a snappy name like me, right? That gets you respect, you know what I mean? So we'll give you a family name. That's a great honour. You got it? Call yourself Tortellini, chum.'

'Your Majesty,' offered one of Capone's gang, 'that's a type of pasta.'

'You know who you is speaking about?' Capone yelled furiously. 'Baby Angelo "Machine Gun" Tortellini. He was my brudda! I calla this dude Tortellini in honour of my dead brudda and you talk about pasta? I hear one more squeak out of you, and you're geography!'

'Erm, are you sure you don't mean "history", Your Majesty?' ventured the rat.

'No, I know what I mean. You're gonna be scattered so far and wide your momma's gonna need an atlas to find you again. You got me?'

The rat gave a little shriek and scampered to the back of the pack and out of sight. Capone put his paw round the robot's metal shoulder.

'You're one of the family now,' he said. 'You just keep pulling the heads off things, right?'

'You got it,' the robot replied happily: a new career beckoned! 'That's where the final shot's going to be made,' he said, pointing up to the Tower of Power in the distance.

'I like shooting,' Capone snarled. 'Let's get this over with, boys.'

Rats, robots and actors converged on the castle like a swarm of moths around a lighthouse. Only less, well, moth-like.

*   *   *

'Stop right there, again, you heinous and evil, deranged, genius-type scoundrel!' demanded a furious hedgehog. He stood at the entrance to Robotnik's improvised laboratory atop the Tower of Power. He could hardly believe what he saw.

The laboratory was a shambolic mess, plainly assembled in a very short time as a purely temporary measure. A huge roof hatch had been opened to the radio antenna. The antenna itself was acting as a lightning conductor, funnelling great sparking arcs of power into gigantic metal coils assembled around an enormous wooden slab, just like the one left behind in the Great Tower. Smoke and steam hissed everywhere, dispersed temporarily by blue electrical sparks which crackled away up massive steel rods every few seconds. Viscous fluids bubbled in great fluted glass columns, bubbles of gas constantly rippling upwards from the bottom of them. Two large emergency generators were bolted to the walls halfway across the rooms, with large metal levers protruding invitingly from them. Robotnik stood by one, Eggor by the other. Between them and our heroes were a squadron of Buzzers, which hovered in the air like a hive of livid bees confronting a shoplifting grizzly bear, and a veritable legion of Grounders, tank-like robots which growled into action the moment the intruders appeared.

Now, all that's pretty neat. But it's not really surprising, and in Sonic and Tails's case that's the effect we're looking for. It was what was on the wooden slab which staggered Sonic and Tails, even though they knew what they might find. It was the appearance of the thing in the flesh, as it were, that really blew them away.

It was, indeed, twenty metres tall. It lay flat on the slab, restrained by metre-thick leather straps around its chest and legs and by metal manacles on its wrists. In short, it was a drop-head HUGE version of Sonic himself. There were, however, some crucial differences, which would have given the game away were the thing not plainly about fifteen times as tall as our plucky blue hero. It wasn't wearing red sneakers, which Sonic was awfully glad about. On the other hand, they would have been something to see, the sort of footwear which gives rise to rhymes about old women who live in shoes. Furthermore, the hedgehog from hell was green instead of blue, and it had horrible scars like zip fasteners around its neck, wrists and forehead. A huge pair of metal bolts protruded from the sides of its neck, begging the question: how big was the spanner which fitted them? A huge metal skull cap was clamped over its head and metal coils connected this to the generators. It was simply too heinous to look at.

Sonic and Tails whizzed to the attack and the badniks rumbled into action to fight them. Frantically, Robotnik and Eggor waited for another crack of lightning to power the bodged-up generator system. As the superdudes slowly but surely wiped out badnik after badnik, Robotnik began to panic.

'We must have more power! Eggor!'

His hunchbacked robotic assistant peered up into the skies. Almost in answer to his robotic prayer, a gigantic bolt of lightning arced into the radio antenna and shot down to the waiting generators. The antenna rig lit up with that dazzling blue-white light much beloved of mad scientists and overpaid special-effects departments the world over, and began to crumple. Its metal struts screamed with stress and then started to fly off it like the buttons pinging off Robotnik's waistcoat the day his laundry robot used too hot a setting in his wash. The rig shook and swayed as if afflicted by an earthquake.

'Now, Eggor! Do it now!' Robotnik screamed. The liquids in the glass columns were bubbling furiously and sparks of electricity lit the room up like daylight. Sonic and Tails

pressed ever closer, leaving a trail of smashed badniks behind them. Together, Robotnik and his assistant pulled the levers on the generators down.

A vast surge of electrical energy powered along the metal coils and flowed into the monster on the slab. Its limbs twitched horribly. Ducking the diving attacks of the Buzzers, Sonic and Tails could only look on in horror as the gigantic torso of the monster commenced straining against the straps holding it in place.

Eggor pulled another lever. The slab seemed to jerk as the monster sat bolt upright and it began to descend.

'It is free! My beautiful creation! Now it will destroy the Green Hill Zone, and your revolting squeaky friends will be destroyed! And then it is your turn, you wretched hedgehog! Ha ha ha! Mad! They called me mad! I who have discovered the secret of eternal life! Ha ha ha haaa!' Robotnik screamed. He fled for the far end of the room, getting as far away from Sonic and Tails as his plump little legs could manage.

Our heroes could only watch helplessly, their path to him blocked by the last of the Grounders, as he hopped into his waiting Egg-o-Matic and vanished into the night. Eggor followed close behind him, leaving in a second Egg-o-Matic of his own.

Sonic and Tails bounced and destroyed the last of the robots and raced to the edge of the opening in the floor. They looked down but saw only a wooden slab far below, its straps and manacles lying in ruins. Frankensonic had come to life, and was surely even now heading out into the night to destroy the Green Hill Zone – and all their poor, innocent and above all unsuspecting friends!

High above them, meanwhile, the rig was in imminent danger of collapsing. The first generator exploded right beside them, a victim of its severely overloaded circuits, soon followed by the others. The heroic pair leapt back just in time to avoid being incinerated.

'We can't follow Robotnik. We've got to follow that monster and stop it!' Sonic yelled. 'Cowabunga! This is a time for real heroism, buddy!'

They leapt and flew upwards as the rig toppled sideways, striking the top of the Great Tower and ploughing into its roof, ripping it away. Inside, they could see Robotnik's laboratories vanishing in the collapse of stonework and a series of explosions as more lightning arced into the tortured metal remnants of the rig. Castle Robotnik was disappearing before their very eyes!

As he flew away, Eggor was full of regrets. The film crew hadn't arrived in time. They must have been delayed coming back from Hill Top Zone, and there hadn't been enough power to use the handful of cameras in the Tower of Power, even if Eggor had had time to grab them from the small video studio in the basement, which he had not. But at least, he thought, we should get film footage of Frankensonic stomping the Green Hill Zone into the dust from that ever-reliable Attenbot, and that will make Master happy. And a happy Master is a happy Eggor. Oh yes!

23

OVER-THE-TOP DERANGED MAYHEM AND MADNESS!

Frankensonic smashed its way through the walls at the base of the Tower of Power as if they were made of tissue paper. It headed for the outer walls of Castle Robotnik and smashed its way through them as well. The homing devices installed in its bizarre home-made robotic brain guided it inexorably towards the Green Hill Zone, and it lumbered onwards, crushing everything in its path.

Behind it, Sonic and Tails flew down to the ground, watching its progress despairingly.

'How can we ever hope to destroy that?' Tails wailed. 'It's just impossibly, totally unbelievably huge! Talk about giving a whole new meaning to the term extra large!'

'We have to think of something,' Sonic snarled in frustration. 'It must have some weak point, somewhere. All we have to do is find it. Surely.' He didn't sound very convinced.

'And here we see the giant monster, *Sonicus Robotnikus Blimminhugius*, out on its nocturnal prowlings,' came a smooth, robotic commentary from somewhere off to their left. 'It is astonishing that such an enormous creature can move so gracefully. It is in search of its favourite prey, small fluffy animals of the night.'

'Gracefully? What is that?' Sonic growled. 'Who is this bogus idiot?'

'And what the fugding heck is *that*?' Tails yelped. Ahead of Frankensonic, a ragged straggle of rats, robots and bad actor-droids was emerging from the gloom of the Scrap Brain Zone's blasted and barren landscape.

'Looks like Capone and his rats,' Sonic said, trying to take it all in. 'But then, not wanting to steal your thunder and all that, little buddy, but what the sugaring flip is *that*?'

He pointed to a swarm of black robots, led by a giant Slicer, which were emerging from all around the castle walls in the distance.

'Right, my lovely badniks, there he is. Melt-down time! Fall in!' the Slicer yelled at full volume, pointing just behind Sonic and Tails. They looked round to see the Spielbot heading towards them.

'What is going on? What's more, what are we going to do?' yelped Tails. 'This is complete and utter madness!'

'Right,' came a robot voice in the general direction of the rats. 'This is Tortellini your director speaking. Keep the wide-angle lens on that monster and save the close-up shots for the heroes.'

'That must be us,' Tails said, puffing his chest out a little. However, the little swarm of cambots that spread out from the robot giving orders seemed to be giving far more of their attention to Capone and the human-shaped actors with him.

Frankensonic, distracted for a moment from pursuing his pre-programmed course of mayhem and carnage, looked down at the frenzied hubbub of activity all around it and lo, it was a bit confused. It stared at one group of little things, then at another, and it couldn't figure out what to do.

It was sure little things featured in its programming, but it seemed to remember having to do a short stroll first. Unfortunately, internecine warfare broke out at once among its enemies.

'Hey!' Tortellini yelled. 'That's Attenbot D trying to steal my movie! Get him, guys!' His robotic film crew sped towards the second unit approaching in the distance. The rats stood around looking confused. Frankensonic turned its attention to Sir Norbert and Thug, who had decided to go out on an all-action glorious-death finale and were charging with their weapons. It raised one immense foot to squash them like bugs, but then it was distracted by yet another group of little creatures swarming towards it.

Even in the pouring rain, they all seemed to be managing to keep their flaming torches burning as they marched on Castle Robotnik. There were literally scores of them. Led by Sally Acorn, the animals of the Green Hill Zone had turned out to help Sonic and Tails. She'd even talked a selection of creatures from the Emerald Hill Zone and beyond into helping out. Johnny, Tux, Joe, Flicky the bluebird, Chirps: they were all marching on Castle Robotnik holding smouldering torches, with Mickey and his monkey friends and a swarm of bats for company.

'As you join us here, it's nine wickets down and twenty overs to go before the close of play,' one of the Cricket Bats commentated. 'All it needs now is a good yorker, leg stump.'

'I don't think so,' Mickey replied, 'I think a good bouncer, at about head high, is just what we need here.' He charged over to where Tails and Sonic were standing amidst the general chaos. The monster looked down vacantly as he passed, its robotic brain unable to handle the thoroughly confused mass of data its senses were feeding into it.

'Get me up to its head,' Mickey yelled to them, waving an electronic screwdriver and an enormous monkey wrench (well, what else would he use?). 'I can dismantle that overgrown piece of garbage.' The fox's twin tails were already spinning. As Sonic and Tails took off with a determined monkey in tow, Tortellini confronted Attenbot.

'And here we see the major problem evolution has bequeathed to the hapless Frankensonic,' the Attenbot went on babbling. 'Its primitive brain is simply not equipped to deal with such complex sets of sensory inputs, and –'

In a masterly piece of television criticism, and providing a lesson of which many more should take heed, Tortellini pulled the Attenbot's head off. His film crew cheered wildly. In the distance, a black robotic killer squad edged ever closer.

'Melt-down time!' the huge Slicer promised, urging them ever forward. 'Ignore these irrelevant vermin,' it continued with contempt in its voice, pointing to the rats in the way.

'Irrelevant vermin, huh? Why, I oughta . . . Suck on this, you dirty rat!' Capone snarled, raising the Ebon Staff of Peaminster the Magnificent like a bazooka and flicking his paws over the *Inferno* setting. The rat gangster almost fell over backwards as a huge cloud of fire billowed from the staff. All that was left when the smoke cleared was a large pile of smoking metal junk.

Up in the air, Mickey grabbed one end of the long stitched line which zigzagged across Frankensonic's forehead.

'It's just like a zip. Fly along it,' he said to Tails. As the flying fox zipped along sideways, Mickey used his paws to unzip the monster's forehead and neatly flipped open the top of its cranium to reveal a mass of whirring cogs and buzzing circuit boards.

'I knew reading *Teach Yourself Brain Control in Ten Easy Lessons* would come in handy in the end,' the monkey commented, completely out of puff with the strain of his effort. 'Sonic, just use yer spanner, me old cock sparrer, and unwind its nut.'

'No sooner said than done,' Sonic laughed. He plunged into Frankensonic's robotic brain and his paws were a blur of whirling action, undoing every bolt he could find.

The monster's eyes crossed and rolled back in their sockets. Clawing frantically at the air, the enormous horror began to totter backwards as a stream of spare metal parts flew from its opened skull. Sonic flew out just in time and the monster staggered backwards. Frankensonic lumberingly staggered and reached almost to the walls of Castle Robotnik. Then it fell like a space shuttle, demolishing what little was left of the place in an instant. Where once Dr Robotnik's castle had stood like a gloomy sentinel at the top of the hill, piles of rubble littered Scrap Brain Zone like so many oversized toy bricks. Everyone cheered wildly.

'Did you get that on film?' Capone growled to Tortellini.

'Don't growl at me. I pulla the heads off things that growl at me, you know whadda I mean?' the robot snarled back; he was really getting into this role.

'Okay, chill out,' Capone said, taking a step backwards. 'Like, how did your boys do? Speaking as one brudda to anudda.'

'They did great, I tell you,' the robot said happily. 'We got you immortalised on video forever, nuking those robots. There's an Eggscar in this for everyone.'

Capone puffed out his chest and the buttons on his jacket almost popped off.

'Hey! Chloe! Come over here and do that fawning adulation bit again, babe,' he ordered. His moll sighed and came walking over to throw herself at his feet. An actress droid in scanty, vaguely medieval clothing stopped her in her tracks.

'Sister, can I have a word with you about gender stereotyping and equal rights?' she said forcefully.

The gleam which lit up Chloe's eyes said that they were the best words she'd heard in years.

24

ALL'S WELL THAT ENDS WELL, DUDES

Back in the Green Hill Zone at last, Spielbot S was making his farewells to Sonic and Tails and their buddies.

'I'm going to be a purely independent movie maker from now on,' he told them cheerfully. 'I have this idea for a movie about an alien who comes to befriend a little hedgehog and reveal the wickedness of our ways to us. I was going to call it *Eggstra-Terrestrial* but I'm sure I'll think of something much better.'

'Wish you well, metallic dude,' Sonic said a little uncertainly. He didn't often converse with robots, after all. Although the Spielbot seemed well-meaning, he wasn't sorry when the robot clanked off into the distance.

'Porker seems to be recovering,' Tails said happily as he stuffed another burger into his face. 'I guess that after we demolished Castle Robotnik we must have destroyed whatever it was that was turning him into a monster.'

'Yeah, that would explain it,' Sonic added sarcastically, knowing there was only a couple of pages left to clear all this up.

'I've been doing a bit of research on that,' Mickey said as he wolfed down another pawful of peanuts. 'On the remains of Frankensonic's brain. I've got a way to go yet, though. You can't learn everything there is to know about Weird Science all in one go, guys.'

'I worry about you,' Sonic said half-seriously. 'Are you totally sure you won't end up like Robotnik? I mean, I don't trust all this tinkering with electricity and brains and stuff.'

'How could I end up like Robotnik? I hate eggs,' the monkey sniffed. 'Give me a decent banana milk shake any day.' With that, he put the striped straw in his mouth and sucked greedily at his long, long glass.

'And here's Sally,' Sonic said happily. 'Hey, Sally, if you hadn't turned up with all our buddies like that, the monster would never have been so confused. And we'd never have been able to get into its brain and destroy it! Good call, my nut-gathering bushy-tailed pal!'

'Well, we all know you're cool hero dudes and every-thing, but sometimes even you can do with just a little bit of help,' the squirrel said modestly. Sonic beamed with pride.

'Yeah, it's like a great leg-break bowler always needs a real fast-reaction man at short square leg,' one of the Cricket Bats said with an air of vacuous profundity. The other Cricket Bats nodded sagely. No one else knew what on Mobius they meant. Having short legs was enough of a problem without them being square as well.

'But I do worry about poor Eggor. I mean, Kevin,' Sally said sadly. Sonic frowned a little. He remembered how, when they'd rescued Kevin the squirrel from his entrapment in Eggor's form before, the pesky squirrel had come awfully close to stealing one of his best buddies away from him.

'Huh! Worry about his missus and all those kids,' he said a little unkindly. 'But we don't know what that major league butt-pain Robotnik may be doing, even if Porker is getting better. What'll he do next?'

'At least Capone may help stop him,' Tails said, trying to cheer Sonic up. 'And he's got those robots with him as well. Tortellini, I think the leader was called. He'll be able to get right up Robotnik's nose.'

Sonic looked rather disgusted. 'Makes him sound like something nasty,' he retorted. 'No, you mark my words. Robotnik will be back with some dastardly scheme or another, and sooner rather than later too.'

'But what does that matter?' Sally said brightly. 'He's tried before and failed. Several times. And we always have someone to protect us. And we all know who that is, don't we everybody?'

'Yeah!' they all cried happily. 'SONIC THE HEDGEHOG!'